ESCORTING THE GROOM

THE ESCORT COLLECTION, BOOK THREE

LEIGH JAMES

CMG PUBLISHING, LLC

Published by CMG Publishing, LLC

Cover Design © 2016 by Cormar Creations

Editing by Red Adept Editing.

Proofreading by Dana Waganer at www.danaproofwrite.com.

LUCAS

"Can you interrupt Mr. Preston, please? Tell him it's his cousin, Lucas. It's urgent." I stalked around my townhouse with my cell phone gripped in my hand. The midafternoon sun shone brightly into the living room. As soon as I got off the phone, I was going out for a punishing run in the Boston humidity.

As if I could outrun what I was about to do.

"Lucas," James said. "This is a surprise. When was the last time I saw you? My wedding?"

"Something like that." I looked out the window, wishing I didn't need to have this conversation. "It's been a long time. How are you? How're Audrey and the kids?" The question felt perfunctory on my lips.

"Great," James said. "Our youngest just started walking. So we're still living in a babyproofed house, but we're getting there."

I felt a headache coming on. "How many kids do you have, again?"

James exhaled, annoyed. "Three, Lucas. We have three."

"That's a lot of kids."

"So what do I owe the pleasure of this phone call to?" my cousin asked, cutting right to the chase. "I'm sure you didn't call to chat about my kids, seeing as you can't remember how many I have."

"Right." I cleared my throat. "It's about my trust…" I let my voice trail off.

"If I remember correctly, it had some pretty specific provisions."

I winced. "Yeah. It's like yours—it's a generation-skipping trust. But mine has some interesting contingencies."

"Such as?"

I gripped my cell phone harder. "Such as… I have to get married before I turn thirty-five. Otherwise, my sister gets everything."

James let out a low whistle. He had no love for my sister, Serena. "That would suck."

"I know. That's the point."

"How old are you?" James asked.

"Thirty-four. And I'm not dating anyone. That's why I'm calling you." I took a deep breath. "I need the name of that agency. The one Audrey used to... you know. Where she worked when you met her." I couldn't bring myself to elaborate any more than that. James's wife, Audrey, was an escort when they'd started dating. It had been the family scandal of the decade, right before the one I had somewhat recently starred in.

"You're hiring an escort to *marry*?" James asked.

"You married one," I said, a bit defensively.

"That's because I fell in love with her, asshole," he barked.

"I didn't get in touch so you could pass judgment." I tried to keep my voice even. "I just need the information."

"When's your birthday?" James sounded as though he'd calmed down. And as if he was laughing at me.

"In three weeks."

He stopped laughing. "Are you fucking kidding me?"

I stared out the window, taking in my penthouse view. The Boston Common stretched out, picturesque and green, in front of me. "No, I'm not."

"Jesus, Lucas. Nothing like the last minute." I pictured my handsome, rugged cousin pacing around his office in Southern California.

"I've been going back and forth about this." I took a

deep breath. "But I can't let Serena inherit all the money in that trust. It's billions of dollars." I winced as I pictured my sister running off between fundraising luncheons to squeeze in another Botox injection. "And I've just run out of time to meet Miss Right."

"I think this is a bad idea," James said.

"It's obviously a bad idea."

He sighed. "The name of the agency is AccommoDating. They're in the South End of Boston. The madam's name is Elena. Tell her I sent you. She always liked me."

"Why do I doubt that?" I quipped.

"Because you're not as dumb as you're acting right now." James was quiet for a second. "You're not really going through with this, are you?"

I coughed. "I don't really think I have a choice. I don't want to ask a friend to do it—"

"Since when do you have friends?" My cousin knew me and my work-obsessed habits too well.

"Right. I'm calling Elena. Wish me luck."

"This is a wedding I don't want to miss. You better send out the invites soon. My kids are playing baseball, and I'm coaching. We're busy, but I'll fit you in."

I promised to keep him posted before I hung up, scratching my head. My cousin, James Preston, had been a bachelor billionaire for as long as I could remember. He was also a real-estate mogul *and* a total prick. The idea of him happily married, with three kids and a babyproofed house, was baffling.

And yet, the inscrutability of his situation paled in comparison to what I was about to do.

~

BLAKE

"I'd like it if you'd stay," Ethan said, trailing his fingers up my arm.

I fell back against his Egyptian cotton sheets. "Of course I'll stay." Ethan was one of my regular Johns. He was funny and kind, and his apartment in the Leather District next to downtown Boston was gorgeous. He always treated me with a high level of respect, more like a treasured girlfriend than a hired plaything.

"Blake, I've been thinking…" He waited until I turned to him expectantly. "What if I put you up somewhere? Bought you a nice apartment? I'd take care of you, baby. You wouldn't have to work for the service anymore. I'd pay all your bills."

I ran my finger along his jawline. "Ah, you're sweet." I smiled at him playfully, trying to lighten my sudden feeling of suffocation. In some ways, it would be lovely to be Ethan's kept woman, to be able to leave hooking behind. But I'd rather make my own money and then retire.

And be alone.

His eyes pierced mine. "I mean it. A nice girl like you? You're the total package. Beautiful. Smart." He tucked a lock of my long blond hair behind my ear. "You don't need to do this anymore. Let me give you a new life."

Ethan was handsome, and he had more money than God, but he hadn't been able to find the right woman to settle down with. "Ethan, that means a lot to me, but I can't."

His brow furrowed in disappointment, but he didn't look surprised. "Why not?"

I sat up and started getting dressed. "I don't do relationships. Not anymore. But I appreciate the offer."

"Did somebody hurt you?" he asked softly.

"Once upon a time, they did." *And no one else was getting an opportunity for a repeat performance.* I shrugged and gave him a small, forced smile.

"That's a shame."

I nodded. "It is." It *was* a shame, but I couldn't go back and change the past. I just had to move forward, the only way I knew how, the only way I wouldn't get my heart broken.

Alone.

"THIS ISN'T your typical assignment, Blake." My boss, Elena, pursed her lips, which were expertly coated in her signature maroon lipstick. Elena was the madam and CEO of AccommoDating, Inc., the escort service where I'd worked for about a year.

"What's ever been a typical assignment? This *is* the escort business, after all." I raised an eyebrow at her. "You're going to need to be more specific. *Way* more specific."

She adjusted the collar of her sleek black blazer. "What if I told you he was offering you a million dollars?"

I opened my mouth then closed it, momentarily stunned. *Holy guacamole.* "I'd ask you what he wanted in exchange," I said, recovering. "'Cause it's gotta be something big."

"The client is Lucas Ford. Have you ever heard of him?"

Lucas Ford was one of Boston's elite CEOs, a technology billionaire. "Yes."

I kept up with business news, reading up on all the latest stocks and business reports. After I paid my expenses and took care of my mom, I heavily invested what remained of my income. I was saving for a future that did not include working as an escort, even though it had proved to be lucrative. "He's a technology mogul, right?"

Elena was pacing now. "Right."

"I read about him in the *Globe* recently. He's in his thirties. Gorgeous, too, if I'm remembering correctly." What I also remembered from the article was that Ford was a venture capitalist who routinely bought and dismantled other people's companies. He didn't do interviews, and he had a reputation for being ruthless. A former employee had said he had "no empathy" and ate up other companies in a "zombie-like fashion." After reading the article, I remember thinking that although he was hot, he sounded like a dick.

And now he was about to become my client. *Great.*

"He's very good-looking," Elena agreed. "He owns several technology start-ups. He's a billionaire from a long line of billionaires. His family, the Fords, is one of the country's wealthiest. They're old Boston-*Brahmin* money."

I twirled a lock of my blond hair, intrigued in spite of myself. "Okay… but what does any of this have to do with me? Why is Lucas Ford hiring an escort, and why is he spending so much money—aside from the fact that he can afford to?" He had to be into some *seriously* kinky shit if he was offering a million dollars. I shuddered.

Elena pulled down her thick-framed glasses to look at me. "He was referred here by his cousin, James Preston. Do you remember I told you one of our girls married her client?"

I nodded. "There was more than one though, right?" Elena often told us about her "success" stories, in which one of her working girls ended up marrying a rich client.

The madam shrugged. "It's happened over the years."

"So what about the cousin? This James?" I asked, nudging her back to the matter at hand. Cinderella stories were great and all, but I wanted to get back to the important part. About the million dollars. The million dollars would be much better than any fairytale—because then I would get to rescue myself, and my mom, and we wouldn't have to depend on anybody else ever again.

Because *that* never seemed to work out too well. For either of us.

"James recommended our service. Lucas doesn't need *just* an escort. He needs someone to..." She started pacing again, no longer looking at me.

"Elena." I was losing patience and my imagination was running wild. "What is it?"

She sighed. "Lucas has a trust. It's substantial. If he wants to inherit it, he has to be married by the time he turns thirty-five. And it has to last." She waved her hand. "I'm not completely clear about the details on the time frame. He mentioned something about a year."

I raised an eyebrow. "He needs a *wife*?"

"That's right. By the time he turns thirty-five."

Both eyebrows rose. "How old is he?"

Elena stopped pacing and turned to me. "Thirty-four and eleven-twelfths. His birthday's next month."

"So you want me to… marry him? Really soon?"

Elena nodded at me. She had the decency to look ashamed.

I, on the other hand, had no such decency. "I'll do it," I said immediately. It felt wrong—the idea of marrying some crazy venture-capitalist billionaire for money—but I *refused* to let myself think it through. That kind of money would change my life forever. And that was what I needed.

Desperation could drive you to do crazy things. I was about to be Exhibit A of just that.

LUCAS

I fought my nerves as Ian, my driver, pulled onto Tremont Street in the South End of Boston. I was rarely anxious, but this afternoon was proving to be an exception. I forced myself to focus on my surroundings. The neighborhood was picturesque, with neat rows of brick townhouses.

Ian double-parked my Range Rover and let me out. I groaned inwardly before I went to meet Elena and my escort, Blake Maxwell. Elena had sent me her picture; Blake was drop-dead gorgeous. Other than that, I only knew that she was blond, healthy, and twenty-eight years old.

And she'd agreed to marry me in exchange for a million dollars.

My heart was heavy as I trudged up the steps. My

parents had drilled it into our heads, from the time Serena and I were children, that we had to comply with the terms of the trust in order to inherit the family fortune. Otherwise, the money would go to some distant cousins.

Serena had already married, thereby complying with the terms of the trust. She'd known exactly what she was doing when she married Robert and divorced him a few years later. She was officially home free, scheduled to inherit billions of dollars.

Unless I took half of them from her.

My mother had been adamant on her deathbed. Get married. Inherit the money and split it with my sister. My mother saw Serena for who she really was: a spoiled, snobbish party girl, interested more in the state of her manicure than the state of the world. *I love your sister, but don't let her get all of it.* Those were some of my mother's last words to me.

That was why I was here: to honor my mother's wishes. Had my sister been a more responsible human being, I would've let her have the trust. All of it. I had plenty of money of my own. But Serena only cared about parties, luxurious vacations, and spending hundreds of thousands of dollars on high-end filler for her face and high-end fashion for her closet. I didn't want to see her sink my family fortune into lip plumper,

Prada boots and donations to her beloved college sorority.

Serena would completely lose it if she knew that Blake was an escort—which was the only thing about this predicament that was awesome.

I walked through the doors of AccommoDating's airy, bright office. A tall, attractive woman approached me, her short hair spiky and highlighted. "You must be Mr. Ford." She shook my hand firmly. "I'm Elena. We spoke on the phone."

"Please, call me Lucas." I nodded at Elena, who looked more like a high-powered corporate attorney than a madam. "I reviewed the contracts you sent over, and everything looks in order. I signed them an hour ago. And I wired the deposit money into the account per your instructions."

"I know." Elena smiled at me. "Please, sit."

I sat down, warily scanning the office for signs of the escort.

"After I take my agency fee, the rest of the money will go to Blake directly," Elena said. "In the interim, as stated in the contract, you are responsible for all of her expenses. Food, clothing, housing. Her terms are complete at your one-year anniversary."

I cleared my throat. "I had my lawyer add one additional term: if I'm satisfied with her performance, she'll get a bonus of another million dollars at the end of the year." I'd decided that was one way to avoid any drama or poor behavior over the next twelve months: offer my escort an additional monetary incentive to behave.

Elena looked stunned. She pulled her glasses down on her nose and studied me. "I'm sorry?"

"I'll pay her double if she does a good job. It's to encourage good behavior," I explained. "That means no excessive partying, no drugs, no boyfriends or extra-marital activity, and she has to be pleasant and appropriate at all times. She can't ever breach the confidentiality agreement. My family has to believe that our relationship is real. If she does all those things for a year, then I'll give her another million dollars. It's worth it to me—this is very important."

Elena opened her mouth then closed it, studying me. "I'll tell Blake that," she said after a moment. "She'll be thrilled."

"Is there anything else?" I cracked my knuckles, antsy, eager to be on my way. "I have meetings this afternoon."

"I'll make sure Blake's ready." The madam got up, hustled to the front desk, and handed me her card. "Please call me if there are any issues. I know that Blake is more than up to the task—she's a true professional, and this kind of money will be life-changing for her."

"Then it's win-win," I said confidently. Inside, I felt anything but. *This is fucking crazy.* What made it even worse? It was all my idea.

But once I made a choice, I acted on it. I followed through. That was how I'd gotten ahead in the high-tech industry, becoming a billionaire in my own right before I'd even turned thirty. I was a venture capitalist, and I was considered a ruthless one: I bought new companies and sold them at whim, never letting personal attachment become a factor in my business dealings. I rarely, if ever, doubted myself. And as I sat in the office and waited for my escort, I realized why: self-doubt was creeping and invasive, a choking weed wrapping itself around my insides.

I roughly brushed the doubt off, eradicating it from my mental landscape. This was just an unfortunate circumstance, a blip on the radar. I was hiring this girl for the greater good. She was going to help me, and I was going to help her.

And then I was going to get back to what was really important: running my empire. Alone.

BLAKE

Elena came hustling through the door, her cheeks flushed, as I put the finishing touches on my makeup.

"Are you all packed and ready?" she asked.

I nodded, gesturing to the luggage I'd neatly assembled over the course of the afternoon. Elena had let me have free range over AccomoDating's wardrobe. I'd packed gorgeous designer dresses, skimpy bathing suits, expensive jeans and T-shirts, and of course, lots of sexy lingerie.

I hadn't packed a wedding dress, though. That was the one thing Elena didn't have. Lucas and I were going to have to figure that out.

I took a deep breath, trying to calm my nerves. I had no idea what sort of women my new client preferred or what his tastes were like. My earlier Internet search of him had come up largely empty, aside from the *Globe* article. There were items here and there about his technology empire, his latest start-up acquisition, and older photos of his proper-looking parents attending various society events. I'd found lots of pictures of his sister, Serena. She was stunning, with long dark curls and the figure of a Hollywood starlet. She appeared to be a lady who lunched, served on several boards, and attended what seemed to be an endless string of black-tie events.

Elena patted my hand, bringing me back to the

present. "The client's added some terms to the contract," she said.

"What?" I asked, immediately suspicious. This close to so much money, I was waiting for the rug to be yanked out from under me—a learned response.

"An additional economic incentive." Elena gave me a reassuring smile.

I didn't want to get my hopes up. "Please tell me what you mean."

"Mr. Ford just told me that if you follow the terms of the contract to the letter for the next year, he'll give you more money."

A nervous flutter went off in my chest. It took me a second, but I finally recognized what the feeling was: hope. "Go on."

"This is big, Blake." Elena's eyes sparkled with excitement. "He said if you pull this off, and the family believes this marriage is real, he'll give you another million dollars at the close of the assignment."

I almost fell over. "Seriously?"

She nodded. "Seriously. You know I don't joke about money."

"Wow… just, wow." *Two million dollars.* For the first time in my life, I was finally going to rise above the poverty line. Not only that, I was going to get the actual *hell* away from it.

"He's waiting," Elena said. "He seems antsy, and he's definitely all business. Not exactly into small talk. But very handsome."

"Works for me," I said, grabbing the over-sized designer pocketbook I'd borrowed from the wardrobe and throwing it over my shoulder. The bag was new; I'd taken the tag off of it that afternoon. It had cost more than my monthly rent, which I found utterly ridiculous. But I had to look the part. I had to seem like a billionaire's fiancée, not an escort hired to pretend to be a billionaire's fiancée. My cheap plastic tote from Target wasn't going to cut it.

"Are you sure you're okay with this? It's a big commitment..." My boss's voice trailed off.

"Don't get soft on me now, Elena." I kept my tone light. The truth was, her concern touched me. "I'll be fine. In fact, I'll be two million dollars more than fine. How many people get to say that?"

I'd already promised myself that if Lucas Ford was mean, or if he was dangerous at all, I would leave the assignment. Money was important, and I needed it badly, but my safety came first.

The money came a very close second.

Elena nodded. "I just want to make sure you'll be okay."

"You don't need to worry about me. I can handle this," I assured her. "It's just business."

She reached out and clasped my hand. "I know how much this will help you. You and your mom can finally get a nice place. Somewhere safe. But I mean it, Blake, if you have any second thoughts, call me. I'm here for you."

"Thank you." I smiled, trying to reassure her. "I'll be fine. And just wait until my mom hears about the money!" I couldn't wait to call my mom, to let her know that by the end of this assignment, we would officially be in the monetary clear. I would just have to get her to swear, up and down, that she wouldn't tell my leech of a sister.

Elena called our bouncer, Ty, and had him collect the luggage. "Mr. Ford's car is out front," she instructed him.

I watched as Ty grabbed the bags and headed out of the back room, carrying the clothes I would be wearing for the coming months as I lived out my days in a stranger's home.

A stranger who was about to become my husband.

LUCAS

A very bulky, menacing-looking man came out of the

back room, carrying two suitcases, his biceps popping. He gave me a warning look as he headed outside.

"What?" I asked, standing up.

"What d'ya mean, *what?*" he asked, his voice as strong and heavy as his body.

"Why are you giving me a death look?" I prided myself on getting to the point.

He stopped and turned to me, not putting the suitcases down. "Blake's my *girl*," he said. "You hurt her, I'll come and find you. You break her heart, I break your face."

I nodded, crossing my arms against my chest so he could see my own biceps, which weren't quite as large as his, but came pretty close. "Well… okay. If that's all."

"Yeah, it is," he grunted, then carried the enormous suitcases down the stairs.

I cracked my knuckles again, but I decided I wasn't going to fight him. Not right then.

More movement extended into my peripheral vision. I turned to see a tall blonde come out, throwing her long hair behind her shoulder and smiling at me prettily. She took my hand firmly. "Blake Maxwell," she said, her voice throaty and pleasant. "Pleasure to meet you."

She looked even better than in her photo. I hadn't thought that was possible.

I shook her hand, absolutely dumbfounded by her

beauty. "Lucas Ford," I said, somewhat stupidly. Her smile broadened, and I caught a glimpse of her white, even teeth. Jesus, she was gorgeous, and nothing about her looked remotely fake. I caught myself wondering what it would be like to touch her skin, to pull her against me.

Down boy, I warned myself. *Jesus.* We hadn't even made it through the front door, and I was ogling her.

Ogling wasn't part of the deal I'd made with myself.

"Well, I'm all packed and ready to go," she said, her voice gentle.

I shook my head as if to clear it. "Great." I turned to lead the way.

But there was nothing great about it. My escort was so pretty, it hurt to look at her. And I was going to have to marry this girl and pretend that it was real, all while keeping my hands to myself. Because that was one promise I'd made. In order to keep my exposure—physical, emotional, psychological—to a minimum, I wasn't going to sleep with Blake.

Not at all. Not ever. Not once.

It was going to be a long year.

BLAKE

The billionaire was cute. Gorgeous, actually, but with the way he'd fumbled when he saw me, he seemed almost puppy-like. I mentally breathed a sigh of relief—I'd been worried what he'd be like since I'd gone back and re-read that article. I took in his curly dark hair, green eyes, and the large muscles going on underneath his dress shirt, which was open at the throat. He was on the verge of being seriously sexy, but he practically tripped down the stairs as he led me to his fancy SUV. Ty was out there, watching us, a smirk forming on his face as he saw me work my magic on yet another customer.

Ty told me he'd come and punch this guy if he turned out to be a freak. I winked at the bouncer as I accepted Lucas's hand and climbed into the back of the car. My look told Ty, *don't worry, I got this.*

And here I'd been all nervous that I was about to be married to a stranger.

I settled into the luxurious leather seat next to my client. Lucas looked at me and smiled tightly. "This is… awkward."

"We'll be fine," I said. I reached over and squeezed his hand. "I'm thrilled about the job. Thank you for the opportunity."

"Wait till you meet my family," he said. "You might

want to hold off on the gratitude. You're going to earn every dollar from this assignment."

"That sounds ominous."

"That was my intention. I'm the nicest one of the bunch." He trained his green eyes on me, and I shivered. A glimpse emerged of the intense CEO who swallowed other companies in a zombie-like haze. "And that's saying something, because I'm not very nice."

I looked out the rearview window, Ty disappearing into the distance. "Oh." My voice came out small. So Lucas Ford *was* a dick. "Great."

He smiled at me again, and I noticed that he had a dimple. Just one, in his left cheek. "I'll make an exception and be nice to you."

My nerves abated. "I'll make an exception and be nice to you, too."

His dimple deepened as he regarded me. "Blake Maxwell, you have a deal."

LUCAS

"Tell me about yourself." I bit the inside of my cheek, wincing. Everything I said seemed ridiculous to me. For someone who didn't do anxious, my nerves seemed to be carrying the day. It must be all of Blake's blond hair, scrambling my brain.

In my real life, I barely bothered with conversation with the women I slept with. But I had to talk to my fake fiancée. I didn't have a choice if I wanted this to seem real, and it had to. If Serena suspected I was just doing this for my inheritance, I had no doubt she would go running to the trust administrator to contest the terms in an attempt to inherit every cent of our family's billions.

Blake shrugged, her movement breaking my reverie. "There's not much to tell. I've been working for Elena for about a year." She said this quickly, as though she didn't want me thinking about her occupation. "And before that, I was a hostess and a waitress at some local restaurants."

"Which ones?" I asked.

"L'Hereux, Demain." Her pronunciation of the high-end French restaurants was flawless. "I worked at Ministry for a while."

"I like Ministry," I offered.

"It's pretty inside." She smoothed her skirt. "Where's your office?"

"Downtown." I seriously sucked at small talk.

"Where do you live?" Blake asked, undeterred.

I jerked my thumb toward the left. "Newbury Street. I have a penthouse suite at The Stratum."

"That's a beautiful building."

"That's why I bought an apartment there. What about you? Do you live in the city?" I asked.

"I live in Southie. And not the nice part." She gave me an embarrassed smile, and for the first time, she seemed like a mere mortal, not some underwear-model goddess.

"I like Southie—even the not-nice part. My favorite diner's there. MiMi's. On Kneeland Street."

She smiled more fully, flashing those brilliant white teeth. "That's my mom's favorite."

"No way. Does she live down here?" I asked.

"She's actually my roommate." Her face softened. "She likes the roast beef hash, which I just don't get. It disgusts me."

"You're crazy. I like it, too. Your mother has excellent taste."

"I'll relay that to her." Blake picked up a lock of her hair and twirled it while I tried not to stare. "So what about *your* family? They're local, right?"

"My father lives in the city with my stepmother." I laughed and scrubbed my hand across my face. "It feels silly to call her that. She's thirty-six."

Blake raised her eyebrows slightly. "How old's your dad?"

"Seventy-six."

"Oh. Huh." She looked momentarily boggled. "What about your sister?"

"Serena. She lives close by, too. But thankfully, I don't run into her too much."

Blake looked at me with sympathy. "Why are they so terrible?"

I shrugged. "You'll see soon enough."

"What's our story going to be, anyway?" she asked. "Do they think you're dating someone already?"

I surprised myself by laughing. "I haven't told them a thing. I'm going to introduce you to them this weekend. I was thinking we could plan a dinner."

"That sounds good... but can you tell me more about your situation? And your trust?" Blake asked. "Elena mentioned something about it, but she didn't go into much detail. I like specifics. I want to do the best job I can for you."

"Good. I appreciate that." I stared out the window as the city passed by. There was a lot of traffic on Massachusetts Avenue, commuters heading back to the suburbs from their downtown jobs. "The trust is from my mother's side of the family. It's a generation-skipping trust, which means that my mother never inherited any of it. It will pass directly to me and my sister if we comply with its terms. The provisions of the trust stipulate that in order to inherit the corpus, Serena and myself both need to be married by the age of thirty-five, and that the marriage must last for at least one year."

"What's the 'corpus'?" She wrinkled her nose. "And why would it have terms like that?"

"The corpus is the bulk of the money in the trust instrument. And as for the terms, it's pretty common to have terms that denote that the grantee is mature enough to handle the inheritance." I scrubbed a hand across my face. "In my case, my mother's family wanted to be sure that the heirs only got access to the money if we were mature enough to take care of it. And they thought that marriage—one that wasn't short-term—

was a good marker of that… or their trust and estates lawyers did."

Blake was quiet for a moment, appearing to process what I'd told her. "You said Serena was older than you?" Blake asked. "Is she married?"

"She was. She's divorced now." I turned back to Blake. "But she's qualified for her portion of the trust. She's met the requirements. The only thing standing in the way of her inheriting the whole thing is me. She doesn't get her money until it's been determined whether or not I'm getting the other half. That's why you're here."

"But otherwise, she gets everything?" Blake asked.

I sighed. "That's right. And if you knew my sister, you'd know why I don't want that to happen."

"I can't wait to meet her," Blake said, deadpan.

BLAKE

We pulled up outside The Stratum, and the valet opened my door.

"Wait a minute," Lucas snapped.

The valet nodded and immediately closed the door.

"This will be the first time we're seen in public."

Lucas turned to me, his green eyes searching my face. "Are you sure you're up for this?"

I nodded. "Absolutely. This money will be life-changing for me. I'll be able to take care of my mom, not to mention what a million dollars would do for me."

"If this works, you'll get two million." Lucas's intense gaze held mine. The outrageousness of what we were doing hung in the air between us.

I smiled at him gamely. He needed to see that I was his ally. "I can do what you're asking, and I'm more than happy to. I promise I'll do what you ask, when you ask. Okay?"

"Okay. Then I should give you this." He pulled out a box and opened it. "We should start as we mean to go on." An enormous, square-cut diamond engagement ring glittered in the box, leaving me breathless.

I stared at it, open-mouthed. "Huh. *Wow*."

"I don't socialize with the people in my building too often, but they should see you wearing the ring. Everyone should."

I ogled the huge ring. "They'll see it, all right."

He took my hand, giving me a solemn smile and simultaneously, the chills. "Blake Maxwell, will you marry me?"

I smiled back at him. This was not how I'd pictured

this moment as a little girl... but since when had my life ever gone as I'd hoped?

"Lucas Ford, I accept." He slid the ring on my finger, and I wondered vaguely whether his driver, who was double-parked and completely silent, thought we were insane. Then the valet opened the door again. I stood on the sidewalk, watching the diamond sparkle in the late-afternoon sun. I remembered the money.

And I no longer cared what anyone else thought.

THE LOBBY of the hotel was as I remembered it. There were marble floors, marble columns, and teak woodwork. It was very luxurious and a bit severe, sort of like Lucas Ford himself.

I didn't tell him that I'd been there before. With other men. I hoped that none of the staff would recognize me. If they did, I prayed they at least had the decency to pretend otherwise.

I tentatively put my hand on Lucas's arm as we headed toward the elevator. If people were going to believe that we were a couple—engaged, no less—there was no time like the present for us to act like one. Lucas shot me a look but then took my hand. Even though I was five-feet-eight, I felt positively tiny next to him as he hustled me through the lobby. He pulled me close against his six-feet-three frame, nodding curtly at the hotel staff, not stopping to say hello to anyone. Lucas Ford was clearly a lone wolf. It was going to be difficult to convince people that he had finally chosen a mate. He released my hand when he got inside the elevator.

"Lucas..." I let my voice trail off. "Would it be okay if I ask you some more questions?"

His green eyes scanned me, making me shiver again. "Such as?"

"Such as, why did you hire me? Why didn't you ask a friend? Or actually..." I let my voice trail off.

"Actually what?" He faced the elevator doors as they opened then strode through. From what I could see, there was only one door on this floor. We had reached the penthouse suite, occupation one.

Now two.

He opened the door, and I momentarily forgot about all of my questions. *Holy guacamole.* Even though I'd been to The Stratum before, I'd never been in the penthouse suite. It had all the usual touches one would expect—gleaming hardwood floors, gorgeous furniture, original artwork. But the best part was the floor-to-ceiling windows that took up an entire wall, overlooking the park. I went over to them and looked out, gaping.

"Wow." The park stretched out before me, its flowering trees and sparkling ponds glinting in the afternoon light. "This might be the best view in the city."

Lucas came up beside me. "I've always liked it." He turned to me. "Now, what were you asking me?"

"I'm asking why you hired me when you have all of this." I gestured to the view, the apartment, and finally to Lucas himself, which brought a small grin to his face. "It can't exactly be difficult for you to find a date."

His eyes sparkled. "It's not that it's difficult. But I need this to be a business transaction. I'm not interested in having a relationship with anyone. I'm certainly not interested in having a wife."

I knew I shouldn't ask more, because it wasn't my business. But curiosity got the better of me. "Why is that?"

"I can see that you're the inquiring type." The small smile still played on his lips. "I'll make you a deal. You can ask me five questions, and I will answer them honestly. But then I get to ask *you* five questions, and *you* have to answer them honestly. And then we're done with all this getting-to-know-you garbage. Deal?"

I crossed my arms against my chest. "Deal." I looked toward the kitchen, mentally kicking myself for starting this. I wasn't looking forward to answering his questions. "Can we have a drink while we play this?"

Lucas immediately headed toward his liquor cabinet. "Hell yes, we can. Does that count as one of your questions?"

"Does that count as one of yours?"

"No." He poured us each a neat bourbon.

"Then no for me, too." I started formulating my list of questions. I knew he wouldn't give me a second chance. I had to make these count.

Lucas sank down onto one end of his enormous leather sectional, and I sat down on the other, tightly gripping my drink. "Okay. Here we go. Question number one: why aren't you interested in having a relationship or a wife?"

Lucas took a sip of his drink. I tried not to let my eyes wander down to the part of his chest visible beneath the undone buttons of his shirt. "That's a compound question. That should count as two questions."

I shook my head. "It's not a compound question because it's addressing one over-arching point. Besides, it's what you just said. Now please stop being so technical, and let's get this over with."

He chuckled and then sat back, looking resigned. "I'm not interested in having a relationship or a wife because, quite frankly, I haven't met anyone who's held my interest for long enough. Not for a month. Not for a year. And certainly not for a lifetime."

He was pretty full of himself, but at least it seemed like he was being honest. "So… question number two: have you ever had a real relationship before?" I knew he'd never been married because I'd done my homework via a thorough Google search.

"Yes. I have had a real relationship before." His brow furrowed, as if I might be giving him a headache.

"Question three: how old were you when you had this relationship?" I had a million more things I wanted to ask, but I was running out of road. I had a feeling this was the only way I would be able to get this information out of him.

Lucas had another sip of bourbon. "I was twenty-eight."

"How long did the relationship last?"

"Three years. You know you only have one question left, right?"

I nodded. "What went wrong with your relationship?"

He looked at me darkly. "And here, I was starting to think I liked you." I could see the muscles in his throat work as he drank some more. "The relationship didn't work because it turned out my girlfriend was a cheater and a liar. She played me. Big time."

"I'm sorry," I said. "What happened?"

Lucas looked at me, his face impassive. "You know you're out of questions."

"I know. You don't have to answer." I took a sip of my drink, dreading my own impending turn on the hot seat.

"I'll answer anyway because you should probably know. She married my father." He laughed and drained his glass.

I just sat there, stunned. *Was it possible that I'd finally met someone with a family as messed up as my own?*

LUCAS

Well, at least we'd gotten *that* out of the way.

I poured myself another drink and splashed some more into Blake's glass. "Liquid courage," I said kindly. "Are you scandalized about my father? My ex-girlfriend?"

Her eyes were huge as she nodded.

"Don't be. I should've seen it coming." I sat back down, taking another sip of bourbon and regarding my fake fiancée. Actually, she was my real fiancée—my head started to swim with the logistics of it, so I pushed the thoughts aside. "Okay, enough chatting. It's time for your questions. Are you ready?"

Blake nodded again, but now instead of shocked, she looked nervous.

"Why do you work for Elena?"

"Because waitressing doesn't pay enough. And I'm taking care of my mom—she's sick, and she's on all sorts of medication that we can barely afford. I don't have a degree. I don't have any real skills. All I have is this." She pointed to her face. "And this." She motioned to the rest of her body.

Ah, her mom was sick. It was sad that she'd had to resort to working as an escort, but I understood. "Question number two: do you have a boyfriend?"

She laughed. "No."

"Question number three: have you ever had a boyfriend?"

Blake stopped laughing and took a gulp of her drink. "Yes."

"You're not really into giving way too many details, huh?"

"Does that count as one of your questions?" she asked hopefully.

"Absolutely not. Question number four: tell me more about your boyfriend—the one you don't want to talk about."

She lifted her chin a little, an almost imperceptible sign of defiance. "What makes you think I don't want to talk about him?"

"It's not your turn to ask me things. Just answer the

question—honestly. I figure that's the least we can do for each other." I drained my glass again.

"He was my high-school sweetheart. He cheated on me after we were engaged. A month before our wedding." Her cheeks flushed. "With my sister."

Whoa. "Your family sounds almost as messed up as mine."

She smiled at me tightly and finished her drink.

My mind raced. "Is this going to be too painful for you—planning a wedding? After what happened? And these don't count as my questions, by the way."

"It won't bother me at all. I was nineteen. Vince and I were going to get married at the VFW. It's not like I get sentimental about it."

I snorted. "Whoever this Vince is, he's fucking crazy. You're gorgeous. Smart. It's not like he could do any better."

"That's sweet," she said. "But my sister has tactics. They usually involve her boobs. And quite frankly, anyone who could be persuaded by her, especially that close to our wedding… I feel like I dodged a bullet."

"So good riddance, right?"

"Good riddance. Right." She looked at me hopefully. "May I please have some more bourbon?"

"Absofuckinglutely." I got up and poured us each

another drink. "This leads me to my final question: are *you* interested in having a relationship ever again?"

Blake eyed me. "No." Her voice was husky. "As in, *hell* no."

I beamed at her. "So this is going to work out great for both of us." I was starting to feel a lot more optimistic about the whole arrangement.

I should have hired a fiancée a long time ago.

BLAKE

It was officially official: Lucas Ford and I were a perfect match. I was glad I knew the truth about him and that he knew the same about me. Now that I'd glimpsed what Lucas was really like, I was relieved. He didn't do messy emotional entanglements. Neither did I. We had a contract. There were strict parameters, and that was all he wanted.

This was going to work out just fine.

"Well, now that we've gotten that out of the way, what should we do next?" I asked, eyeing the tanned skin peeking through his shirt.

Lucas checked his watch. "I'm going to go to the office for a few meetings. You can do whatever you like. Relax. The whole apartment is yours, and no one will bother you. You can get settled in. And when I get back, we could go to dinner," he watched my face. "...if you'd like."

I smiled at my client. "That sounds great."

"The other thing we have to do," Lucas continued, looking grim, "which will be infinitely less pleasant than a quiet dinner, is to reach out to my father and my sister. They need to meet you sooner rather than later."

"When?"

"Tomorrow." Lucas looked as if he was talking about arranging a meet-up with the local firing squad. "We need to face this head-on."

"You're right. When's your birthday? When do we have to..." I let my voice trail off, uncomfortable saying the actual words.

"We have to make it official in three weeks." He smiled at me. "Maybe that's another thing you can do this afternoon."

"What's that?"

"Plan our wedding."

I TOOK the liberty of exploring the apartment once Lucas left. It was enormous, with views of the Common and the shops on Newbury Street. I'm sure it had cost millions. I couldn't imagine what it would be like to be able to afford a home like this. To have a life filled not only with beautiful things, but with the security of knowing no one could take it away from you. Because you owned it. And because you were free from the vagaries of being poor and worried about it all the time.

I went into the master bedroom and trailed my fingers across the sumptuous four-poster bed. I got to live here for a whole year. Then I would have enough money to buy my own apartment—nothing like this place, but something nicer than I'd ever lived. Someplace safe for me and my mom. I shivered, not believing my luck.

That was because I never had good luck.

I called my mother as I sunk down on Lucas's big bed. I had to make sure she was okay and had everything she needed. She was used to me being out on assignment a lot, but this was going to be a much more difficult separation. I wasn't going to be able to see her while I was working for Lucas. Elena had made it clear: no one could know about my family and my real background. It hurt to know that my mother wouldn't be allowed to attend the wedding, but I was being ridiculous. It wasn't a real wedding, anyway. So why did it matter?

She picked up after the first ring. "Mom," I said cheerfully.

"Hi, honey!" she exclaimed. "I'm so glad you called. How's everything going? Are you on your new assignment?"

"Yep." I kept my tone light.

If someone had told me that I would be working as a high-end escort someday, I would've said they were crazy. If someone had told me I would be living with my mother and that she not only knew what I did for a living and but also tolerated it, I would've told them they were flat-out out of their mind.

Mom hated what I did. She cried when I'd finally broken down and told her the truth about where the money was coming from. She was too sick to work, and her government assistance didn't even cover her medication. We were in between a rock and a hard place. The rock was the streets. The hard place was AccommoDating. When I told her that we really didn't have a choice, it was the truth. It had taken some adjusting, but she'd finally made some sort of peace with my choice. She never wanted to know specifics, and we rarely talked about what I was doing.

Which was obviously fine by me.

"How are you doing? Did you do your treatment today?" She sometimes forgot to take her medications and do her treatments. That was going to be the hardest part about being away for so long. I would ask my sister to check on her, but I didn't trust Chelsea to follow through and keep an eye on her.

"Yes, honey. You left me the daily list, remember? I open up the calendar every day, and I do everything on the list, just like you said. I'm going to be fine. Don't you worry about your mom."

"I always worry."

"I know you do! That's because you're my little worry wort!" She laughed. "So... is this thing you're doing going to work out? Are you going to be gone for as long as you thought?" She gingerly sidestepped any details.

"Yes. I'm at the client's house. We signed a contract. He's very nice—he even likes the hash at Mimi's Diner."

"Well, I approve of at least *that*," my mother said.

"He's a gentleman—you don't need to worry about anything." I took a deep breath. "He's going to give me even more money," I said. The words came out all in a rush. "He's going to give us so much money that we're never going to have to worry again. We can buy an apartment. Someplace nice. We'll be able to get all your medications and everything. From now on. You don't have to worry about anything ever again."

"Oh, honey... really?" I could tell she was close to tears.

"Really. I promise. It's going to be so great, Mom." I felt on the verge of tears myself, and I struggled to calm down. Ever since Vince had jilted me, I didn't do emotions, and I certainly didn't do out-of-control ones. I didn't want to completely freak my mother out by crying. "But listen. You can't tell anyone about this. And if you see any pictures of me in the newspaper or anything else like that, you can't show them to anyone, and you can't talk about it. Understand?"

"What pictures in the newspaper?" She sounded alarmed.

"Mom. There aren't any pictures—yet. But my client is a successful CEO. He comes from a lot of money. There might be pictures of us in the *Globe* or the *Herald*." I swallowed hard, not wanting to tell her the whole truth. "I just want you to be prepared."

"Blake Walker Maxwell, I can tell you're keeping something from me. You tell me what's going on right now!"

Oh boy. She meant business—she'd broken out my middle name. That was almost as bad as her asking me for a pinky promise, which was probably coming next. I sighed, not wanting to tell her the truth but knowing that in the end, she was going to find out, anyway. It might as well be now. "I'm going to marry him."

She was silent for a beat. "I'm sorry?" she finally asked. "What did you just say to your mother?"

"I said I'm going to *marry* him. That's the job."

"I don't understand this. What does that even mean?" She sounded bewildered.

"It means that he has to get married for financial reasons," I explained, trying to stick to easy talking points. I didn't want my mother to get distressed or upset about all the details, and I knew they would be confusing to her. "So he hired me to marry him. There will probably be an announcement in the papers, so you should know."

"So you marry him, and *then* what?"

"We're going to live together for a year. After that, the assignment is over, and he's going to give me more money. A lot more."

The silence was deafening, although I knew she hadn't hung up. Yet. "I don't know about this," she said finally. "I've let you get away with working for that lady for too long. You can't marry someone for money. And after what happened with Vince..." She let her voice trail off.

"Mom, I'm fine." I pressed the phone against my ear, wishing I could reach out and hug her. When I'd found out about Vince and my sister so close to the wedding, I'd fallen apart. My mom had been there to pick up the pieces. The pinpricks of tears stung my eyes. I didn't want her to worry about me anymore.

I heard her start crying. "I just want something better for you."

"I knew you'd be upset. That's why I didn't want to tell you. But please don't worry. This is going to be *huge* for us… and it's just a business transaction. My client is a nice guy in a tough situation. I'm helping him out, and he's paying me to do it. And he can pay me so much that you and I never have to worry ever again, okay? So this is a good thing. A *great* thing."

She sighed. "I just want my beautiful daughter to be happy for once. Is that too much to ask?"

Now, it was my turn to sigh. "Your beautiful daughter is happy with the money she's making, okay? Can we please just concentrate on that?"

"How much money?" She sounded suspicious, but slightly less teary.

"Two million dollars," I whispered. "Can you believe that?"

She whooped. "Holy guacamole!"

"Right? Now can you stop being so overly emotional?"

"Definitely not!" I could hear her crying and laughing on the other end of the phone. My mother held a lot inside, but I knew how worried she always was about our situation—whether we would be able to afford groceries the next week, or which medications she was going to have to give up. This was going to change both of our lives for the better.

But there was one last detail to take care of.

"There's one other thing, and it's crucial," I said after she calmed down. "*Please* don't tell Chelsea. If she hears that I'm making that kind of money, she'll be all over this like a vulture on a steaming animal carcass." My sister had taken advantage of both me and my mother one too many times. Not to mention that she'd stolen my fiancé, who she'd subsequently taken advantage of by marrying, divorcing, and collecting alimony.

Even though I didn't mind what she'd done to Vince—he'd thoroughly deserved it—Chelsea was not my favorite person. She would only get a dime of this money if it was over my dead body.

And not even then, if I could help it.

My mother clucked her tongue. "Of course not. You know I wouldn't do that."

"Okay. But I mean it—don't let her talk you into anything." My mother and Chelsea weren't close, but my sister still knew how to work her when she needed something. When Chelsea came begging, my mother often gave her a handout, sometimes at the expense of buying her medicine.

The thing was my sister knew it. And she always took the money, anyway.

"I promise." Mom was quiet for a second. "Do I get to... visit you? Meet this man? Come to the wedding?"

"No. I'm sorry. Nobody can know about my family or who I really am. I won't have anyone there."

"That's too bad," she said.

I grinned into the phone. "You know what? It's totally fine. We're going to be millionaires, Mom! For once in our lives, everything's finally going to be okay!"

"Woo hoo!" I could almost hear her grinning.

"Woo hoo is right!" I hung up with a smile on my own face. Then I proceeded to fire up the laptop Lucas had left for me and start researching venues where I could marry my handsome, brooding, aloof billionaire fiancé.

LUCAS

"I told you to close the deal," I snapped at Simon, one of the young entrepreneurs who worked for me. I was engaged in my usual yelling routine, but honestly, my heart wasn't in it today. I was thinking about Blake. I was pleasantly surprised by our question-and-answer session. I never spoke of Elizabeth and my father's relationship. It wasn't something I liked to dwell on. But it had felt good to tell Blake the truth and to know that she'd been burned before, too.

We were quite a pair.

The downside of that was becoming apparent to me. As I pretended to listen to Simon whine about his deal falling apart, I couldn't stop thinking about her. She was unbelievably gorgeous. She also seemed intelligent and kind—the total package. The guy that had cheated on her was an idiot. I didn't care how hot her sister was.

On one hand, it was good that I found her appealing. That would help our first appearance as a couple in front of my family seem authentic.

On the other hand, I needed to snap the fuck out of it and get her out of my head.

"Go ahead, Simon. I'm listening." I left him on speakerphone, jabbering and whining, while I went and jerked off in my office bathroom. My arousal was inconvenient, but it was only an erection. I dealt with it. And if I let myself fantasize about Blake—writhing in ecstasy beneath me, her hair tumbled across the bed—no one had to be the wiser.

Afterward—after I'd come, hard—I washed my hands and calmly regarded my eyes in the mirror. *Don't be a fuckup. You're going to marry her, and then live with her for a whole year.* It needed to be a hands-free relationship. If we started having sex, and she ended up in my bed every night…

That sounded *way* too much like a relationship to me.

"What did you just say?" I snapped at Simon as I zipped my fly and hustled back into my office.

"I was *saying*, the Nexus Group is trying to get out of the terms—"

"You know what? I don't care," I interrupted. "You're fired. I can't deal with your whining. All you're doing is spouting off a bunch of excuses and giving me a headache. I'm not paying you to do that."

"But, sir—"

I hung up before he could start sniveling. I punched in the number for Shirley, my assistant. "Shirley."

"Yes?"

"You're probably going to get a call soon—"

"From Simon in La Jolla? He's texting me now." She was quiet for a minute, probably reading. "He's pretty upset. Said you just fired him for no reason?"

"Oh, there's a reason." I wished I hadn't drunk so much bourbon earlier. My head was starting to throb. "He just screwed up another deal. Get him lined up with HR. Tell them to give him the usual severance package and send him on his way. Please."

"You know this is the fourth person you've fired this quarter?" Shirley's voice contained no judgment. She knew how to handle me. She was just reporting facts without drama, which was why I paid her well, and why she was the employee who'd been with me the longest.

"We need to fire the headhunters, too," I said. "They keep sending us losers. I want you to start working with HR and form an executive search committee. You can vet the applicants. You'll do a better job than anyone else. We can talk about your increase in compensation tomorrow. Right now, I have to go."

"Mr. Ford, it's only six o'clock." Shirley sounded dumbfounded. With so many deals happening on the West Coast, I usually worked until at least nine every night. And I came in at four in the morning so I could conduct business for an hour with my Chinese associates.

"I know. I have a date." I never talked about my personal life at work, largely because I didn't have one. "With my fiancée."

"What?" Shirley whooped. "You're *engaged*?"

I cleared my throat. "That's correct." Might as well start spreading the news.

"Oh, Mr. Ford, I'm so glad!" She hung up and came barreling around the corner from her office. Her short legs moved in a whir, as fast as a cartoon character's. She stood in front of my desk and clapped. "Do you have a picture? What's she like? Can you bring her in? When're you getting married?"

I held up my hand to stop her. "Easy, Shirley." I took out my cell phone and scrolled to the picture the madam had sent me of Blake.

"Oh, my," Shirley said in awe. "Is she one of those Victoria's Secret models? She looks just like one!"

I indulged her with a smile. "No. But she is pretty,

isn't she?" It seemed ridiculous, but pride bloomed in my chest.

Shirley, who had maybe seen me smile three times in the past ten years, patted my arm approvingly. "She's beautiful. I hope you two will be very happy together. Are you planning a large wedding?"

"That's what we're going to discuss at dinner tonight. But no matter what we do, I hope that you will join us at the ceremony. I would love for you to meet Blake, and for her to meet you." I grinned at my assistant, but I was mentally kicking myself. What the hell was I saying? I was inviting my staff to my fake-but-legal wedding? And I was *smiling* about it?

For fuck's sake.

"Oh, Mr. Ford!" Shirley's eyes glittered behind her glasses. "I'd be honored."

My stomach sank. It didn't sound like Shirley would be forgetting about the invite anytime soon.

I let her cluck and coo for another minute before I said a hasty goodbye and hustled out of the office. I'd made dinner reservations, and I wanted to change first.

I had a very important date.

BLAKE

I twisted the straps of my dress nervously. Lucas had called and said he'd made reservations for seven. His voice was stern and sexy on the other end of the line. Anxious, I'd started getting ready at five, wanting to make sure I looked perfect.

And not daring to think about why.

I was looking forward to tonight. I was looking forward to talking to my client about our wedding. That was crazy, right? Still, I'd looked online at some venues today and had braved a few bridal websites. I'd found some beautiful dresses. Some of the pictures were so dreamy, with the models looking as if they were actual princesses. Even though the wedding was only pretend —pretend for real—I intended to have fun with the planning. I surprised myself with that. I never had fun. Fun and I did not coexist.

I smoothed the fabric of my long black dress and studied myself in the mirror. I looked good. But who wouldn't, wearing a dress that cost six hundred dollars? Elena always kept designer clothes available for high-end assignments like this. She wanted us to be able to fit in when we accompanied our clients to upscale functions and restaurants. She wanted us to look the part.

The dress was tightfitting through the chest; it had spaghetti straps and went all the way to the floor. I had curled my hair in loose waves and pulled it all over one shoulder. I was wearing enormous cubic zirconia studs in my ears. If anyone saw me in this dress, on Lucas Ford's arm, they would never doubt that the earrings were real. They wouldn't question a thing.

I certainly looked the part of the billionaire's fiancée. Still, I couldn't wrap my brain around the fact that people actually lived like this. That women could spend hundreds of dollars on a single dress and live in an apartment that cost millions, overlooking the park. When Lucas paid me at the end of this assignment, I was going to buy a simple, safe condominium in a nice neighborhood. I would still buy my clothes from Target and Marshall's, like a normal person. Who needed a dress like this in real life?

There was a knock on my door, and Lucas stuck his head in. "You ready?" His eyes traveled over me slowly and I flushed. "I'm going with yes. As in hell yes."

I laughed. "Then you'd be right."

"I like being right. I also like that dress." He opened the door and gestured me out. "And I'm starving."

"Me too," I admitted. I'd been so nervous about the job, then so busy settling in and researching wedding options that I'd barely eaten. Bourbon was the only thing I'd had all afternoon. My stomach howled.

"You didn't even have to say it. I can read your mind. Or at least hear your stomach." He smiled and held his hand out for me, and I tentatively reached for him. "I'm sorry I left you locked in here all afternoon. You know you can come and go as you please, right? And help yourself to anything in the kitchen?"

The truth was, I'd been too afraid to leave the apartment. I was worried I wouldn't be able to figure out how to get back in, and I hadn't really known what to do with myself. "I know. Thanks." I grabbed my clutch, and we headed toward the door.

Lucas was wearing a dark suit over a white button-down shirt, open at the throat. He looked impossibly dashing. His dark curls glittered in the early-evening light, and a five-o'clock shadow covered his square-cut chin.

"Where are we going?" I asked.

"My favorite restaurant in the North End. Do you like Italian?"

My mouth started to water. "It's my favorite."

"You know what, Blake? We have more in common than I'd hoped." He led me into the elevator, and I noticed that my heart was pounding. I tried not to think about what was going to happen after dinner…

"I told my assistant that I was engaged today." Lucas looked a little sheepish. "She was… excited, to say the least. Can we invite her to the wedding?"

"Of course." I felt oddly touched. "I had the chance to look at some different venues this afternoon."

"Great. Tell me about them over dinner. You look beautiful, by the way."

I flushed in pleasure. As soon as the doors opened, Lucas pulled me through the opulent lobby. Several of the guests and hotel staff stared at us. We must have made a tall, attractive, expensive-looking pair.

"Ian." Lucas nodded to his driver, who was waiting out front. "North End, please."

I thrilled at the way the city looked from inside Lucas's luxury SUV, riding high above the heat and humidity of the streets. It was still light at seven o'clock. The summer day was stretching out, long and languorous. "So… how was work?"

"We sound like an old married couple already." He laughed, seeming more relaxed than he had that afternoon. "It was fine. I'll actually have to be going back in soon." He checked his watch.

"You mean after dinner?"

"Yeah. I have to speak with some of my Chinese colleagues. The time difference makes it necessary to go in at odd hours." He shrugged. "It's not a big deal. I'm not much of a sleeper."

I felt a little crestfallen, knowing that he would be heading back downtown instead of the penthouse. Part of me was getting curious to see that chest of his and find out what else he had going on underneath that suit.

Part of me just wanted to get it over with, because the first time with a new client was always awkward.

"How many hours a week do you usually work?" I asked, trying to redirect my thoughts from the gutter.

"Most of them." He smiled, and I noticed again that he had a dimple. Just the one. "What about you?"

I was taken aback. "Um... do you really want to know the answer to that?"

"We're business partners, remember?" Our eyes locked for a moment. "But we don't have to talk about it if you don't want to."

"I don't want to," I said immediately.

"Is it that bad?" His gentle tone surprised me.

"You don't have to feel sorry for me," I said.

"I didn't say I felt sorry for you."

I turned away, but I could still feel him watching me. "It is what it is. Mostly I see it as a means to an end. Otherwise, I just try not to think about it. The money's decent—at least I've been able to take care of my mom."

"That's good," Lucas said, and I heard no judgment in his voice.

I hoped he was done with questioning me. *Most awkward conversation ever.*

We pulled up outside a beautiful brick building. Soft

lights illuminated the name, *Mio Fratello*. I turn to Lucas and grinned. "This is my favorite restaurant. They have the best olive-and-pasta appetizer thingy. I *love* it."

"That appetizer *thingy* is my favorite, too." He was cute when he teased me, not at all like a zombie who guzzled the brains of unassuming technology companies.

"You're gonna have to order your own," I warned. "I'm not sharing."

He agreed. "I doubt you'll ever see me share food. And I would *never* share that. It would be a sacrilege."

We climbed a winding staircase to the second floor and went inside. The *maître d'* bowed slightly at us. "Mr. Lucas. Ms. Maxwell. Right this way." We were definitely getting the Lucas-Ford-billionaire treatment. I'd been there before with a client, but no one had ever called me by name. The host led us over to a private corner table overlooking the street. Candles lit up the room as the sky darkened.

"I'd like the wine that I had set aside," Lucas told the *maître d'*.

He bowed slightly. "Of course."

"You had wine set aside?" I asked. *Who does that?*

Lucas arranged his napkin on his lap. "I don't leave the office much. When I do finally have time to go out, I like things to be as nice as possible. As soon as possible."

"Do you call ahead to Mimi's in Southie to reserve your hash?" I laughed. "I can't really picture Mimi catering to that."

A sparkle lit Lucas's green eyes. "Mimi likes me. She might even tolerate that sort of entitled behavior from the likes of me."

I was going to give him a smart-aleck response, but I became too engrossed in the menu. I was definitely going to have that appetizer, as well as pasta Bolognese, and quite possibly an heirloom tomato and mozzarella salad. Lucas might have to roll me out of there, but it would be worth it.

The sommelier came over with the wine, brandishing the label to Lucas, who barely paid attention. He was so wrapped up in the menu, he didn't look up. "It's perfect," he snapped. "Just pour it."

The wine was poured, and the server beat a hasty retreat.

"You know, you were just sort of rude to that man." I wrinkled my nose. I didn't want to cross a line with my client, but at the moment, he seemed largely unaware of himself and his surroundings. The former restaurant worker in me felt it necessary to speak up.

Lucas calmly looked up from his menu. "I wasn't rude. I was just to the point."

"You're the boss," I said, but I made sure my tone conveyed my displeasure.

Lucas raised his glass in a toast. "To my beautiful, smart, and caring fiancée, defender of sommeliers. Feel free to do all the ordering for me for the next year. I can't stand it."

"Fine." I took a sip of wine, which was of course exquisite.

Lucas regarded me over his glass. "I didn't mean to be rude to that man. But that's the problem—people think I'm being brusque, but really, I'm just trying to get shit done."

"I forgive you on his behalf."

Lucas raised an eyebrow. "I didn't say I was sorry."

"I forgive you on his behalf even though you didn't say you were sorry." I raised my glass and clinked it against his.

"Fine."

I smiled at him, hoping I hadn't crossed a line. "Fine."

"So… please tell me what your Internet research yielded today. Where are we celebrating our nuptials?" Lucas smiled at me now, that one perfect dimple making its appearance, and relief flooded through me. I wasn't on emotional probation. *Yet.* I needed to watch my mouth.

"For such short notice, the local options are pretty

limited," I explained. "We could get into the Ritz or the Four Seasons, but only on a weeknight. What do you think about that?"

Lucas waved the waiter over and gestured at me to order. After I finished, I looked at Lucas. "And the gentleman will have..."

Lucas gave the waiter a forced look of pleasantness for what I assumed was my benefit. "The olive-and-pasta appetizer. And the veal porterhouse." He closed his menu and turned his attention back to me. "Next time, just order for me."

I smiled. "It'll be my pleasure. I just have to figure out what you like."

"I could get used to this. You're just like a personal assistant. A really hot one." He looked down after he made that comment, concentrating on swirling the wine in his glass. "So..." he continued after a beat. "The Four Seasons or the Ritz on a weeknight? We could do that."

"You also mentioned your property up in Maine," I said. "We could have an outdoor wedding there. I contacted a few catering companies in Seal Harbor that would be able to accommodate us on short notice. The only issues with that are hotel reservations and house rentals for guests who are coming, because there aren't a lot of options up there. Speaking of, how many guests were you thinking you wanted? When I spoke to the event planners today, I guessed about one hundred people. What do you think?"

"I really don't have many people to invite. My father and his wife, my sister, Shirley from the office… my cousin James and his wife Audrey. Other than that, I would probably need about fifty or so spots for other family, work friends, a buddy of mine or two from college." He raised his eyes to meet mine. "What about you? We really can't invite anyone from your family…" He let his voice trail off.

"We can't. Elena made it very clear that I couldn't have any relatives present for any part of this." I pursed my lips. "I hope your family doesn't think it's suspicious that I'm not going to have anyone at our wedding."

Lucas nodded. "We'll have to put more thought into that. It can't look strange. Okay, besides Maine and Boston, are there any other options?"

I nodded. "I took the liberty of exploring venues in Vegas, although I imagine that would be considered a little tacky by your family's standards. However, there are several hotels out there that could accommodate us on short notice, and obviously, food and lodging wouldn't be an issue. Neither would flights."

Lucas looked thoughtful as he sipped his wine. "Vegas, huh? I kind of like it. It might horrify my family, which is fine by me. Oh, by the way, we're having dinner with them tomorrow night. So be prepared to suffer alongside me."

My stomach plummeted in dread at the thought of meeting his father, his stepmother/ex-girlfriend, and his filler-faced sister. But then the waiter came over with my first course, and I forgot all about my trepidation, occupied instead with my appetizer. "Perfect timing." I began to eat, closing my eyes for a moment in ecstasy over the flavor. The tartness of the green and black olives contrasted with the tomatoes and the *Gemelli*. The tastes balanced each other perfectly. "Mmmm. That's just as good as I remembered. Better, even."

"It's perfect."

I looked up and realized that Lucas was watching me. He hadn't even had a bite.

I shivered in response. "You should have some." My voice was chiding, but I felt a slow heat creeping over me as I held his gaze.

He looked down at his plate, breaking the moment. "Listen... I didn't mention anything about this to Elena, but we should be clear about something."

Was this the part where he revealed that he was into BDSM, or that he was a furry—i.e., someone who liked to dress up as an animal before he had sex? Lucas might actually be cute dressed up as a bunny...

"Blake?" Lucas interrupted my train of thought, which was probably a blessing.

"Sorry—I spaced out for a second," I said. "What were you saying?"

"I'm not requiring physical contact as part of our arrangement. I meant it when I said that this was strictly a business arrangement."

I thought my hearing might be going. "I'm sorry?"

He looked back up at me, chewing his food thoughtfully. His green eyes glittered in the candlelight. "I said that I'm not asking you to have sex with me as part of this deal. That's not what you're here for."

I swallowed some wine.

"Don't take it personally," he cautioned, watching me warily.

"This *is* strictly professional for me," I reminded him. "And my ego's big enough that I'm not going to take that as a rejection."

"Good girl." Lucas grinned at me. "I just don't want things to get any more complicated between us."

"I understand." I knew I should be relieved, but I felt a small sting of disappointment.

I looked at his broad, handsome face and the stubble forming across his chin. I had another sip of wine. I had wanted to find out what he had going on underneath his suit. "But if at any point something changes, please understand that physical contact is part of my job. And I'm sure your *own* ego is big enough that you know it wouldn't be the worst thing that ever happened to me—if you *did* change your mind."

At that, Lucas gulped his wine, and I grinned at him playfully. Because really, at this point, what did I have to lose?

LUCAS

"You flatter me." The truth was that I was more than flattered; I started to get aroused, becoming rigid from her compliment. "But I mean it—I think this arrangement is going to be mutually beneficial for both of us. I'd like to keep it as professional as possible." I willed my traitorous cock to fall in line.

She nodded. "Whatever you say, boss."

"Can you stop calling me boss?"

"Of course. Sir." She smiled at me, teasing.

The rest of our meal was subdued, spent discussing the pros and cons of each wedding venue and arguing about who had ordered the better entree. Dinner with Blake was, of all things, pleasant. I patted her hand as we pulled up outside of The Stratum. "I'll see you at some point tomorrow. Dinner with my family is at six. Ian's at your disposal, so feel free to go shopping or out to eat, whatever you like. I left a credit card for you and some cash in the kitchen. There's also a gym in the basement of the hotel, which you're free to use. Housekeeping keeps me stocked with food and wine. Please help yourself."

"That's really nice of you," Blake said. "I appreciate how generous you're being. The article about you in the *Globe* didn't do you justice."

"What—you don't think I'm a self-serving, ruthless egoist?" I grinned, oddly touched that she'd read up on me. "With a zombie-like appetite?"

"That's the one."

"See? You *do* flatter me. Most people take that article as gospel." I reached over and squeezed her hand again then pulled away quickly. "See you tomorrow."

The valet opened Blake's door. "Good night," she said. I'm pretty sure I flattered myself by imagining that her tone was wistful.

And with that, Blake headed toward the lobby, alone. I watched her easy stride, her blond hair flowing past her shoulders. *Down, boy,* I thought, but I only felt my erection thicken. *Great.* I was going to be jerking off at work again.

But that was better than the alternative: sleeping

with Blake. Because then I would *really* never get her out of my head.

My cock didn't care about all that. It wanted to tell Ian to turn around so that I could go back and take Blake to bed. *What the actual fuck of my own making,* I thought, as we headed back downtown.

It was going to be a long year.

"WHAT DO YOU MEAN, meet your *fiancée*?" my father roared.

"I mean just what I told your assistant: I'm engaged. You will be meeting Blake, my fiancée, tonight at six p.m. Feel free to bring my step-monster. She's included in the reservation. Oh, and Serena will be there as well. Should be fun." I hadn't felt this giddy since I'd made my first billion and considered myself financially independent from my family.

"Since when do you have a fiancée? Since when do you have a girlfriend, or even go on a *date*, for the love of God?" My father sounded exasperated.

"As you know, I took some time off from dating after Elizabeth left me for you." It didn't hurt my pride to say it out loud anymore. "But seeing as I'm in my mid-thirties, I thought it would be the appropriate time for me to settle down and start thinking about a family."

My father scoffed. "And to inherit your trust."

"And to inherit my trust," I agreed. "The timing's perfect. I'm in love, Blake said yes, and now I finally get the money intended for me. You don't have a problem with that, do you? Seeing as it's not your money in the first place?" Franklin Ford was affluent in his own right, but my mother's family's vast wealth far eclipsed his.

My father clucked his tongue. "Of course I don't have a problem with it. I just want to make sure that you're doing this for the right reasons."

I started laughing; I couldn't help myself. "Suddenly, *you're* worried about the right reasons?" My father and I had never really discussed what had happened with Elizabeth. It was simply that one day she was my girlfriend, and I was happy—at least I thought I was—and the next, she'd moved in with my widowed and extremely wealthy father.

The same year my mother died.

I'd had to do some soul-searching for the reason she'd done it. I was wealthy in my own right, I was young and attractive, and I'd even been reasonably attentive to Elizabeth. But she always liked to be naughty. She always wanted to do the "bad" thing—sex in public places, she wanted me to spank her, stuff like that. I thought it was sort of hot until I realized, after she left me for my father, that what my girlfriend had was a classic case of daddy issues.

I guessed he did something for her I couldn't. I preferred not to think about it any further.

"Son, I know the topic makes you uncomfortable—"

"Oh, please, *please* don't try to talk to me about it now. It's been years. I resigned myself to the fact that you're a dirty old man who married my ex-girlfriend when my mother, your *wife*, had just passed away." That was the thing that upset me the most. I hadn't stopped mourning my mother, and my father had moved on at warp-speed. Time-warp speed.

He sighed. "Someday, when you're a lonely old man, you might understand. Besides, I know you don't believe this, but Elizabeth and I love each other. Very much."

"Can you excuse me for a moment? I just threw up in my mouth. I need to go rinse it out."

My father grunted. "Are we really doing this tonight? And will you be able to be civil to Elizabeth?"

"Yes, we're really doing this. I'm getting married. Soon." I surprised myself by actually smiling as I thought of Blake. "And I'll be civil. I think I'm actually going to enjoy it."

BLAKE

The day stretched on forever. I went to the gym, I made my bed, I took a shower, I stared out the window… a lot. I called my mom to make sure she was okay. We chatted for a few minutes, and she caught me up on what was going on with our neighbors as well as the latest on her soaps. She didn't mention my sister, and I wasn't sure whether that was a good or bad sign. But I didn't bring Chelsea up, either. My mother sounded calm and healthy, and I saw no reason to get her riled up.

I would have cleaned the house, but it was already immaculate. I would've stocked the fridge and gone grocery shopping, but there was already organic food packed neatly on the shelves. I went out for a short walk through the park, but I just felt restless, aimless, as I watched young families playing with their children, and tourists riding the swan boats.

What the hell do rich people do all day if they don't have to work? Or clean their house?

I wandered back to the penthouse and searched for something to read, cursing the fact that I'd left my Kindle at home. I'd been right in the middle of this book about a sexy, rugged treasure hunter who was an ex-Navy SEAL. The only books Lucas had on his shelves were business tomes and biographies. I finally grabbed one about the founder of Berkshire Hathaway and managed to concentrate on it for a few hours.

Then I reached the next stage of my day: widespread panic about meeting Lucas's family at dinner.

I tore through the outfits I'd packed, looking for something that would be attractive but also appropriate. I didn't want my boobs hanging out as I sat across the table from Lucas's father and ex-girlfriend. I did another Internet search on his family, and I ascertained that his father was a silver fox, a handsome and healthy-looking seventy-something. His wife, Elizabeth, was stunning. She had long auburn hair and porcelain skin. I pushed aside a twinge of jealousy as I studied her picture. It didn't do me any good to be jealous of my fake-fiancé's ex-girlfriend-slash-stepmother.

Finally, I looked at pictures of his sister again. Serena Ford was stunning as well. She had Lucas's curls, but she wore them long and loose over her shoulders. Long dark lashes framed her stunning green eyes, so similar to her brother's. I noticed in each of her pictures that she was dressed meticulously, her designer clothes hugging her curves. Serena appeared to have attended every charitable event in Boston for the past five years, always looking flawless. Then I came across her wedding announcement from years before: *Serena Ford, Society Princess, Weds Robert Heathman, ER Doctor.* There was a detailed description of her schooling: Miss Porter's, a post-graduate year at Proctor Academy, Sarah Lawrence. Robert's family was wealthy and prominent; Robert was a graduate of Harvard Medical School.

I briefly wondered why they'd divorced as I sat down on the bed and let out a shaky breath. *I am so out of my league.* I quickly ran through my fabricated backstory, so I felt somewhat prepared: I'd attended public high school and graduated from the University of New Hampshire. Compared to the Ford family, even my alter-ego was a nothing from nothing. But that was at least better than the truth: that I was a hooker pretending to be Lucas's fiancée. *Yeah, that'd go over even better!*

Finally, I calmed down enough to get dressed. I chose a black fitted sheath that was covered in lace. It had cap sleeves and a high neckline. I put it on and checked myself in the mirror; it was perfect. Fitted but not too showy. Classic. I checked the price tag before I removed it. *Eight hundred dollars.* I almost passed out. No wonder it was perfect!

I put my hair up in an elegant bun and was very restrained with my makeup. I inspected myself when I was finished and felt impressed. I looked like a gorgeous billionaire CEO's fiancée. Which I suppose I was. Sort of.

By the time Lucas got home, I was pacing in the living room, trying to resist the urge to either bite my nails or guzzle a bottle of wine. Or both.

He let out a low whistle as he came through the door. "You look stunning," he said simply.

"Thank you." I melted toward him a little. "Of course you know that you look stunning, too."

He loosened his tie and shrugged off his jacket. He flashed me a smile, punctuated by that dimple. "Of course I do. But I don't mind hearing it."

"Are you ready for tonight?" I could hear the nerves in my own voice.

"You've got nothing to worry about." Apparently Lucas could hear them, too. "We'll take care of my family. I'm going to try to enjoy myself." He poured himself a bourbon, and I watched him curiously.

"Do you always need liquid courage to prepare yourself for an enjoyable evening?" I asked. "And, um, can I have some, too?"

Lucas held out the bottle to me, but I groaned and shook my head, thinking better of it. He knocked his small drink back in one sip. "I always need a drink before I see my family. And I told my father we're engaged. He sounded as though he was about to pop a blood vessel."

"Was he… okay?" I asked. "Eventually?"

He shrugged. "He'll live. I didn't give him any details about the wedding because we still have to finalize that. But I'm going to let them know that it's next week."

I stumbled a little. "Next *week*? I thought you wanted to do it in three weeks. I haven't tried to book anything for that soon."

Lucas regarded me casually, the way only a billionaire planning last-minute nuptials could. "We'll figure it out. I can call in some favors from people who owe me if we do it in Maine. Or there's always Vegas. You can do pretty much whatever you want in Vegas so long as you're willing to pay for it. And I am."

"I've been thinking about that... about Vegas."

"What?"

I shrugged. "Don't you think your family would think it was a little, um, beneath them?"

He stalked toward the refrigerator and pulled out a bottle of wine, then poured us each a glass. "Probably." He ran his fingers through his hair, making the curls spring up, slightly out of control. "Let's see how they behave tonight. Then we'll decide what we're going to do."

"Okay." I was nervous, though, because planning the wedding was *my* assignment. One week was a bogglingly small time frame. "Are you sure you don't want to just elope? On an island somewhere?"

"I wish we could—which reminds me, we're taking a one-week honeymoon after the ceremony. I've already cleared my schedule. I'm taking you to an island where no one will bother us."

"Uh… okay." Had I been bored this afternoon? I now had to plan a wedding and prepare for a tropical honeymoon in the course of one week. I had so many items on my to-do list, I was starting to lose track. "And why can't we elope, again?"

"The same reason we have to go on a honeymoon. The same reason we have to meet my family for dinner tonight. This has to seem completely real. Otherwise, Serena will be sprinting off to the trust administrator to contest my inheritance so fast, you'd think she was trying to qualify for the Olympics."

"Okay." I sighed. "I understand."

Lucas's green eyes searched my face. "Do you? We have to go soon. Are you really ready for this?"

I nodded bravely, feeling as though we were indeed about to meet the local firing squad. "Of course. I'm a professional, remember?"

"I remember." He came closer, close enough to touch, and electricity crackled between us out of nowhere. My breathing sped up as I inhaled his scent, something masculine and spicy that wasn't cologne. "And that's good, because I'm going to have to touch you tonight.

Hold your hand and kiss you. Do you think you can handle that?"

I swallowed hard. *Oh yeah. I could handle that, all right.* "Yes, sir," I said demurely.

He cocked an eyebrow at me. "So we've gone from 'boss' to 'sir,' huh?"

I started laughing, and the tension broke between us. "I have to call you something."

"Try honey. Or baby. My sister's a stickler for details." He stepped back from me and headed for his room. "I'm going to change. Start thinking of pet names."

"Right away—*baby*," I said.

He wasn't facing me, so I couldn't be sure, but I thought he might have been laughing.

LUCAS

It was a good thing I'd jerked off properly because Blake looked amazing in that dress.

I pushed the thought roughly from my mind, choosing instead to concentrate on the neat row of suits hanging in my walk-in closet. I selected a light gray one, perfect for a hot summer evening. I also had a feeling that things were about to heat up with my family. Keeping my cool was very important.

I clasped her hand as we strode through the lobby. People stopped to stare at Blake, and I tightened my grip on her. *Keeping my cool, indeed.*

"We're going to *La Ciel* for dinner," I told Blake as Ian navigated the SUV through light traffic. "Have you been there?"

"No, but I'm guessing I'm in for a treat," she said. "It's always voted one of Boston's top restaurants."

I leaned back against the seat and watched the buildings go by. "It's nice. It won't compare to our dinner last night, but it's still serviceable."

"Nothing can compare to our dinner last night," Blake said dreamily. "I keep thinking about that appetizer."

"Me too. I love that thingy." I grinned and she grinned back at me. I felt an urge to reach out and touch her, to run my hands down her bare arm. I probably should—we would be at the restaurant in less than ten minutes, on display for my family to scrutinize and dissect. I tentatively put my hand on hers, surprised and annoyed at the shock that went through my body when I touched her bare skin.

Blake looked down at my hand. "Practicing?"

I retreated to my side of the car. "Sorry."

"Don't be silly." She took my hand and brought it back over, placing it directly on her thigh. I squeezed her leg. It felt smooth and muscular under my touch. Then of course my cock stirred again. *The traitor.*

"I take it you're not normally demonstrative with your dates," Blake said.

"I'm physically demonstrative with the women I take home," I offered.

"Ha. But we need to be serious. Would it be okay if I took the lead with our physical contact? I'm comfortable touching you, holding your hand, rubbing your back, kissing you."

"I think that would absolutely be okay." This was getting better and better… except for the fact that I was going to end up with the bluest of blue balls by the end of the evening.

She smiled, pleased with herself. "Good. I think it seems in character, and your family would expect that."

"I appreciate that," I said, "and I think it sounds like a good plan. You take the lead with the affection. I'll take the lead explaining how we met… how did we meet, again?"

Blake trailed her finger down my arm and put her hand on top of mine. I had a feeling she was enjoying herself. I wasn't sure if she was teasing me, making me ache for what I told her I had no interest in. If she was, it was working.

Good thing I was stoic. And stubborn as hell.

"We met at a cocktail party for one of your new technology launches, remember?" she asked. "I worked at a design firm that helped with your branding. We started talking and haven't been apart since that night."

I squeezed her thigh again, deciding to just go with it. "How long ago was that?"

"Six months," Blake said smoothly. "And now we've decided to make it official."

"I know my sister will be researching you online as soon as we've paid the check tonight. What's she going to find?" Elena had assured me she'd taken care of every detail with respect to Blake's identity, but as we got closer to the restaurant, my nerves began to hack into my overall system.

"Elena put up a fake website for the design firm with my profile on it—it has my picture and everything, including my fake degree." Blake whipped out her phone and pulled up the site. "See? The company is fictitious, but it looks completely legit. It says I'm currently on a leave of absence to plan my wedding. And there's no other trace of me online. AccommoDating has a members-only, secure website. All of my information's been taken down, and she had our tech guy make sure you couldn't find residual links online anywhere."

"Well… good." I scrubbed my free hand across my face, imagining other areas of vulnerability where my sister might strike. "What's the story with your family?"

Blake didn't miss a beat. "My mom died of cancer. My parents divorced when I was very small, and I never knew my father. And I'm an only child, so that's it. Just me, and no aunts or uncles to speak of, either."

"No mother-in-law, hmmm? You really might be the

perfect woman," I teased. She just smiled and went back to stroking my arm.

I went back to talking my erection down.

La Ciel was elegant and crowded, but my surroundings barely registered with me as I gripped Blake's hand and headed for the table where my family was already assembled and waiting. It figured. They probably had a pregame strategy session. "Are you ready?" I asked Blake lowly.

She smiled and nodded. "No," she said, under her breath. "But I'm already pretending."

"I like it." We reached the table, and my sister's eyes almost popped out of her head at the site of the tall, beautiful woman at my side. "Good evening. Serena, Father, Elizabeth." I nodded at them all politely. "This is my fiancée, Blake Maxwell. Blake, this is my family." I pulled out the chair for her, and she descended onto it slowly, like a queen.

They positively gawked at her.

I took the opportunity to inspect them. My father looked fit and tan, as though he'd just played eighteen holes, which he probably had. Elizabeth, my stepmother, looked as though she'd had some work done recently. Her skin was pulled more tautly than usual, and her eyes slanted upward almost painfully. She was still attractive, but now her face had an unnatural, feline-like appearance underneath her auburn waves. Serena glared at me from beneath her dark tumble of curls. Her perfectly painted red lips contrasted with the light tan she'd acquired during some fundraising weekend on Nantucket.

She hadn't told me she'd gone, because I hadn't asked her. I'd seen the picture in the society pages and flipped past them quickly, tired of her endless photo opportunities, her unyielding desire to be the center of attention.

"I'm Franklin Ford. It's lovely to meet you," my father said, a bit too enthusiastically. He shoved his hand at Blake across the table and shook hers animatedly. "I'm so thrilled that you and my son are getting married! Wow. Just look at you." He proceeded to do just that, his eyes sparkling as they roamed her body.

Then he leaned underneath the table to check out her legs.

I cleared my throat and shot a knowing look at Elizabeth, who was turning a dull, scary shade of red. "That's enough, Dad. I appreciate you being friendly and all—but you don't need to be *quite* so enthusiastic."

My father popped back up and gave me a sour look. "Jesus, Lucas. You haven't even been here for a minute. Say hello to the family and have some wine before you start complaining." He turned to Blake. "I apologize for my son. He can be a little crass."

"I hadn't noticed." She smiled at my father.

"I'm sorry." I interrupted what was clearly my father's preamble before he started telling Blake all about my flaws. "I know you're just excited for me, Dad." I turned to the ladies. "We're all just excited. Right, Elizabeth? Serena?"

"Absolutely," said Elizabeth, her eyes raking over every visible inch of Blake. "It's nice to see that you're finally going to settle down after all this time." Her smug tone was unmistakable: *after all this time without me,* it insinuated.

I clenched my hands into fists under the table. Blake must have felt me tense because she started to rub my back soothingly. "It's really nice to finally meet you all," she said, her tone friendly and naïve. "Lucas has spoken of his family so highly."

Serena raised a meticulously waxed eyebrow at Blake. "*Really?* You're going to pull an 'aw-shucks' routine on us? With a body like that?"

"Huh?" Blake blinked at my sister, her eyes widening. "I'm being polite. Because we're just meeting, and because this is a happy occasion."

"Don't bother with the manners." Serena rolled her eyes. She was wearing a tight black dress that showed off her surgically enhanced breasts. An enormous gold Rolex watch glinted against her wrist.

"Oh, Serena, what's the matter?" I asked. "Feeling outfoxed?"

"Hardly." She scowled at me. "It's more that I'm suspicious. I haven't seen you all year. None of us have. And then, three weeks before I'm set to inherit the trust, you spring *this* on us?" She pointed at Blake, as if my fiancée was something ugly and dangerous that had slunk out of a sewer pipe to join us for dinner.

I leaned across the table toward my sister. "Are you sad that you're only going to be inheriting half of the family fortune now?" I whispered, conspiratorially. "Or just that Blake's naturally gorgeous *and* much nicer than you?"

"I don't know what you're talking about. There's no such thing as a real blonde." Serena sniffed, eyeing Blake's roots. "And as for the money—you're only getting it after you've been married for a year—and *if* this is actually real, not some sort of sad attempt at fraud." She turned back to Blake. "So, speaking of fraud, how exactly did you meet my brother?" I winced at how shrill she sounded. Mother would have hated to see her like this.

I looked around the table, from my father to my hired bride-to-be. Mother would probably have hated to see all of us like this.

Blake smiled bravely at Serena. "I worked at a design

firm that helped Lucas with his branding. We met at a launch party. I'd like to say it was love at first sight, but that… just sounds so cheesy." She sounded demure, but as she continued rubbing my back, her hand started to go lower, skimming my belt.

I shifted in my seat. *What is she playing at?*

I gave her a quizzical look, but she ignored me, continuing to trace her fingers along my lower back. "I don't think it sounds cheesy," I said. "In fact, that's exactly how I felt." I gestured to my father, who was staring at Blake as if she were an ice-cold drink in the middle of the Sahara Desert that he wanted to guzzle. "I'm just lucky she felt the same way about me."

"I'll say," my father exclaimed. Then he cursed as Elizabeth sharply elbowed him.

"We started dating, and Blake moved in with me shortly after that," I explained. "Since I'm not getting any younger, and we decided we'd like to start a family—"

"Oh, will you stop with your bullshit?" Serena looked as if she might lunge across the table at me. "You do *not* want a family. You can't even stand to be in the same room with children! This is all for show. There was no insta-love, and this woman is *not* really your girlfriend."

Blake stubbornly held up her left hand and pointed at her ring. She looked as if she were about to burst into tears. "His fiancée," she reminded Serena, her voice swollen with hurt. Her lip quivered.

My father leaned across Elizabeth in order to better glare at my sister. "Stop making our guest upset," he commanded. "It's nice to see your brother finally happy. Maybe you could start working on that."

"Maybe you should mind your own business," Serena snapped.

"You need to back off," Elizabeth said, coming in between them, her tone nasty.

"Don't start that step-monster routine with *me*," Serena threatened.

Blake shot me a surreptitious look, as if to ask, *are they always this bad?*

I nodded at her, drained my glass, and motioned for the waiter. "Keep it coming," I said, pointing to the empty bottle of wine. Then I froze.

Blake's hand was trailing to the waistband of my pants again, skimming the top of my ass. "Can I have some more, babe?" she cooed when the waiter brought the bottle back. Her sexy voice made my cock jump to attention. I grabbed the wine out of the waiter's hands and poured it for her myself.

"Thanks." She gave me a fuck-me look then leaned over and kissed me, with tongue, causing the muscles all over my body to shiver in response.

My cock jolted again and as we parted, I noticed that all three of our dining companions had stopped arguing and were staring at us, open-mouthed.

"You're blushing," Serena said to me, sounding disgusted.

I jerked my thumb in Blake's direction. "It's her fault. She does that to me."

My father looked positively ribald as he bit into his salad. "You don't say, son," he mumbled through his Bibb lettuce.

Seemingly satisfied with my physical reaction, Blake refocused her attention on Serena. "Now, back to what you were saying about us not being in love—why would you say that? I don't understand."

Serena's head looked as if it were about to pop off. "Since you refuse to stop pretending—even though you're both seriously terrible at it—I'll break it down for you. I'm sure you know that Lucas is on the verge of inheriting lots of money—"

Blake pulled her shoulders back, bristling. "That might be true, but he makes lots of money, anyway. Because he works very, very hard."

"Thank you, baby." I threw my arm around her and pulled her against me. Now that she'd practically grabbed my ass and stuck her tongue in my mouth, the physical lines I'd drawn around us seemed penetrable.

Penetrable. Huh. I was really going to need to work on my inner word choice.

"It's so nice to finally have someone in my corner." I squeezed her against me as I looked pointedly at the faces across the table from us.

Serena drained her wine glass, looking simultaneously frustrated and disgusted. She ignored me and spoke directly to Blake. "He only gets the money if he's married by the time he's thirty-five and *if* it lasts for a year. But it has to be *real*. He can't just be doing it for the money. You, either."

Blake ran her fingertips over the rim of her wine glass. "No offense, but how would you verify that? That someone's marriage is *real*?"

Serena arched an eyebrow, one of her signature, snotty moves. "I have my ways."

"Maybe I should go back and question Robert," I said, referring to her ex-husband. "And ask him how real *your* relationship was."

A glimmer of something, possibly the real human emotion of hurt, flashed in Serena's eyes for a moment. But it disappeared so fast, I assumed I'd imagined it. "You go right ahead. What Robert and I had was real, no matter how disappointing he turned out to be." Serena had packed her husband off when he began suggesting, on a regular basis, that she quit the Boston social scene and either focus on a career or on having a family. Or both. I'd always liked Robert, but he'd pushed my sister too far.

Serena sat back in her seat, taking us both in. "Let's get back to you two because you're the ones on the hot seat. Not me. I paid my dues and complied with the terms and spirit of the trust. The only way that you're getting that money is if you do the same. I can and will run a background check on you, Blake. You're too stunning to never have graced a society party before. I can check to see if you've received any money or property in exchange for marrying my brother. I'll see if any legal documents have been filed at the Registry of Deeds—if Lucas has gifted you any property, for instance. I could also check to see if any large sums of money have been transferred from his accounts."

I leaned forward, wanting to smack the smug look off of her face. "You'd need a subpoena to check my accounts, and you know it. Good luck getting one."

"I don't need luck," Serena said. "I have a team of top-notch attorneys that I'm going to put on this. They'll find a way."

I sat back in my chair and put my arm around Blake. "I wouldn't spend all that money on legal fees, seeing as you're only getting half of the inheritance you've been expecting."

A pulsing vein appeared on my sister's forehead, and I wished it would pop. "Don't you start threatening *me*—"

"Not only are you being rude, you're jumping the gun a little bit, my dear," my father told Serena, interrupting her. "They haven't even gotten married and hit the one-year mark yet. No one gets the money until then. Not even you."

"Except I would be inheriting the money in three weeks if he wasn't pulling this," Serena said, indignant.

The server brought our entrees, but none of us ate. We all just pushed our food around angrily, the atmosphere crackling with tension.

"We're getting married next weekend," I finally said, breaking the awkward silence. "You're all invited, of course."

"Great," my father said. His eyes sparkled as he looked at Blake, probably imagining dancing with her. *I was so not letting that happen.*

"Wonderful," Elizabeth said, sounding as if she were enjoying the latest family scandal. She was probably relieved there was finally some bigger news than her leaving me to marry my dad.

"Why bother inviting us?" Serena asked. She stood up and angrily shoved her chair against the table.

"Because I, unlike you, care about this family. And I

would like your blessing." I wasn't sure how I managed to keep a straight face, but I did. It was almost impossible for me to care about the family since my mother had died and everyone had shown their true colors. But my sister's blessing, or at least her belief in the truth of the marriage, was exactly what I wanted. What I needed. "I'll send you an invite, anyway. Do what you want with it."

I wanted to add that she was more than welcome to shove it, but since I needed her approval or at least the absence of her disapproval, that seemed ill-advised.

"Well, I'll be there for everything. Every last moment. Because I'm going to catch you in the act, little brother." She tossed her curls over her shoulder dramatically and turned to Blake. "Good night. I'd say it was a pleasure, but you actually just gave me a headache."

Blake didn't miss a beat. "It was nice to meet you, too."

After Serena rage-grimaced one last time and hustled out of the restaurant, we engaged in awkward small talk with my father and Elizabeth until the check blissfully arrived. "I've got it," I said, waving them off. "And I'll be in touch soon with the wedding details."

Before they left, my father hugged Blake more than necessary, and Elizabeth's complexion went molten again. When they finally walked out, I drained my wine glass in a silent, thankful gulp. When we were finally alone, I turned to Blake. "See what I mean?"

She nodded. "They're tough."

"Why were you putting your hand down my pants, anyway?" I raised an eyebrow at her.

She shrugged demurely. "I wanted you to stay alert. And to seem like you're into me." She looked up at me through her lashes. "You don't mind, do you?"

I shook my head. "It worked."

"Good." Blake smiled. "We need to stay on our toes. Speaking of which, dinner made me think about what you said about the wedding."

"Which thing?"

She bit her lip, looking guilty. "That your family would hate the idea of a Vegas wedding."

I grinned at her. "Are you thinking what I'm thinking?"

She nodded, her eyes sparkling.

"They deserve a spectacle." I filled our glasses with the rest of the wine and raised mine in a toast. "To Vegas, baby."

She clinked her glass against mine. "To Vegas."

BLAKE

Lucas was quiet on the ride home. "That must have been stressful for you," I said, trying to draw him out. He needed an ally against his family, and it looked as though I was all he had.

He shrugged, looking out the window. "I wasn't expecting anything different."

"Have they always been so..." I searched for a word that was fitting but not too insulting. "Dysfunctional?"

He shot me a look. "Yes." He was quiet for a moment. "No. I don't know."

I waited to see if he would go on.

Lucas scrubbed his hands over his face. "They were all better-behaved before my mother died. Elizabeth at least had the decency to wait to jump ship to my father's bed a respectable few months after that."

"Oh. Wow."

He chuckled darkly. "She's a piece of work, all right. But my sister… she was still married when my mother died. Robert was a nice guy."

"So why does Serena seem to…" I didn't want to finish the question.

"Hate me?" Lucas's eyes twinkled in the dim interior of the SUV. "Because she said that I was our mother's favorite. And once Mom was gone, there was no one to keep her in line. My father was too busy sticking it to my ex to notice that Serena had gone off the deep end. She got her boobs done this year. She does Botox all the time. She's thirty-seven, for Christ's sake. Too young to be doing that, and too old to be out partying like she is."

"That's too bad. So she's… jealous? It just seems so petty."

"Why did your sister go after your boyfriend?" he asked gently.

I arched an eyebrow at him. I really wished we were back playing pretend in front of his family so I could run my hands down his backside and put him in his place—under my spell. "Are you analyzing me?"

Lucas's gaze held mine. "Aren't you analyzing *me*?"

I shrugged. "Maybe."

"So, back to your sister. Her motivation was?"

"Chelsea. Her name's Chelsea." I swallowed hard.

"She's pretty easy to analyze. If I had a toy, she always wanted to take it. When it came to Vince, things were no different."

"Exactly." Lucas patted my hand. "It's because you're better than her and deep down, she knows it. Same thing with my sister. Serena doesn't want to see me inherit that money because she thinks I've led a charmed life and that I don't deserve any more than I've got. She doesn't understand why I work so hard when I already have so much."

"Why do you work so hard when you already have so much?" I blurted the question out and then I sat there, cheeks reddening, as Lucas gave me a long look.

"You're doing it again. Analyzing."

I nodded at him meekly, worried I'd gone too far.

"Well doctor, let me lay it all out for you." He gave me another long look, but there was no anger in his eyes, just a glimmer of something I couldn't quite put my finger on. "I work all the time because business is what I'm good at. When I started out, I was surprised at how easily it came to me—seeing a company, assessing it, telling early on if it was a good investment. When something comes naturally to you like that, it... feels good. And it's a lot less messy than other things that could occupy my time."

"Like people?" I asked. I couldn't help myself.

"Exactly. Like people. Like my sister." Lucas didn't deny it and he didn't miss a beat. "I don't want to see her inherit all of the trust because she's *never* worked—she's completely out of touch with the realities of the world. She'll spend the money on outfits and trips to Dubai. Give money to her sorority so they'll name a wing after her. That's what she thinks is important in life."

I wanted to ask more about just him, to dig deeper into why he liked to hide in his downtown office and rule his empire from behind his desktop. But he'd switched gears on me and I had to keep up. "But what's wrong with that?" I asked, focusing on Serena. "I'm not trying to disagree, but it's not like she's spending the money on something terrible, something that's going to hurt someone."

"You're right." He shrugged. "There's nothing wrong with it, per se. But my mother would have wanted some of that money to help people. She left the discretion to us, to donate as we saw fit. But my sister isn't interested in that. She'll give money to her pet projects and her alma maters, but she won't do any actual *good* with it, which is in direct opposition to my mother's wishes."

"Why won't Serena honor her wishes?"

He scrubbed a hand across his face. "Because she thinks poor people are disgusting, lazy abominations."

"Oh," I mumbled.

"My sister puts the 'ass' in 'class'."

"Ha ha." But my stomach was sinking.

Lucas looked out the window. "My mother wasn't like that. She believed that we had a responsibility to take care of those less fortunate. I believe that, too. Serena simply thinks that poor people or homeless people need to get jobs. She's incapable of seeing the larger picture—in other words, she lacks imagination. She couldn't dream of a scenario where a person might be forced to make choices that are less than ideal."

I shivered, his words hitting home. I could only imagine what Serena would think of me if she knew the truth.

"I know what you're thinking," Lucas said, his voice low.

I bristled. He was starting to get on my nerves with all of his goodwill and insight. That *Globe* article never mentioned his philanthropic side, which I found disarmingly attractive. "Since when did a reclusive, anti-relationship billionaire like you get so intuitive?" I preferred to keep my own dysfunction, my own problems, below the radar. So I could pretend they didn't exist, like a normal person.

"I don't really like to be around people, but understanding them is part of my business." He loosened his tie and unbuttoned the top buttons of his dress shirt, relaxing against the leather seat. "But back to my sister—talking about her makes me see it clearly. I think we should mess with her. Exploit her weaknesses to our advantage."

Now he sounded like the combative CEO I'd come to expect. "How can we do that? And isn't it dangerous? Don't you need her on your side right now, or at least, not against you?"

"I can accomplish that in part by keeping her off-balance. Serena likes things orderly and controlled. She's not going to get that from us. I'm going to call Elena in the morning."

"Elena? For what?"

He smiled, flashing that dimple. "I'm going to hire some of your coworkers to come out to Vegas."

"Really?" I asked, oddly touched. I hadn't let myself think about it, but I'd been sort of dreading being completely alone at the wedding.

"Really. It'll keep things interesting, and it'll be nice to have some guests on your side of the aisle. And some bridesmaids. But they're going to have to keep up a united front pretending, so that no one knows who they—and more importantly, you—really are. Do you think they can do that?"

I nodded. "They're professional pretenders. That's what they do." I thought of several of the girls I worked with who were a little wild. They could and would pretend to be friends of mine, but that rowdy streak couldn't be disguised easily. "That's really nice of you. But don't you think your sister's going to freak out? With all the, er, riff-raff hanging around?"

A small smile played on his lips. "It wouldn't be the worst thing that could happen to her. But I know what is, and I'm going to do that, too."

"You're full of surprises," I said. "Care to let me in on that last one?"

"First, I'm going to see if I can pull it off. Then I will surprise and delight you with my ruthless ingenuity." His eyes glittered in the semidarkness, and I admired the handsome, rugged planes of his face. I had no doubt in his ability to accomplish what he set out to do.

Not a one.

LUCAS

"Well, good night." Blake and I were in the hallway of my penthouse, getting ready to go our separate ways.

"Are you heading back to the office?" she asked.

I shook my head. "I'm off tonight. And tomorrow, actually. We have some things that we need to attend to."

"Oh? Like what?" She tilted her head up at me in a way that was both attractive and annoying. Attractive because she was beautiful, and annoying because it was the perfect angle for me to kiss her. I wondered if she was attempting to prove something to me again, like when her hand had skimmed over my belt earlier.

If she was trying to get under my skin or make me want her, she didn't have to work so hard. But this was a business arrangement that I wouldn't allow to fail, and I wasn't going to complicate it by letting things get physical between us. Because if I did that—if I did *her*—I would push her away afterward. I was a one-and-done sort of fellow. And I didn't know if she had the emotional wherewithal to deal with that, then live with me and pretend everything was great for a whole year afterward.

I took a step back from her. *Nope. No way. No how.* I didn't do self-destruct. I wanted this to work, and I wasn't about to let my dick get in the way.

Still, Blake was looking up at me expectantly, with her shiny blond hair and her perfect pink lips, which were slightly parted. She knew what she was doing—tempting me.

"Why're you looking at me like that?" I finally asked.

She tossed her hair and licked her lips. "Like what?"

Yeah, right. "You're giving me a fuck-me look again. Why?"

Blake promptly closed her mouth and stood up straight. "Sorry. I was trying to see if you wanted to, *you know*. Just get it out of the way."

"I told you I'm not interested." The lie sounded harsh as it hung in the air between us.

A flicker of hurt might have passed over her features, but it was gone before I could be certain. "Then I'll stop trying to make it easy for you." She smiled at me as though my rejection had rolled right off her back.

I took a step toward her, inhaling her scent. It was her hair; it smelled fantastic. I wanted nothing more than to wind my hands through it, throw her over my shoulder, carry her to my giant bed, and bury myself inside of her. Explore her body. See her breasts freed from the tight bondages of her prim lace dress. Run my hands down her naked skin.

Christ, I was getting hard again. *Down, boy.*

"It's not like I don't want to." My voice came out husky. I allowed myself to trail a finger down her arm, relishing her responsive shiver. "But I told you before: I don't do complicated. And I can't imagine that anything good could come from us compromising the integrity of our agreement."

Blake watched my finger with fascination as I trailed it back up her arm, which was raised with goose bumps. "Just one question about that." She still watched me but sounded alert and focused.

I let myself wrap a hand around her arm, stroking her. My cock was getting treacherously hard. "What's that?"

"Why would sleeping together complicate things?" She sounded genuinely curious. "You and I are both adults. We've agreed to a business arrangement. If we have sex, it would be just that—an extension of the agreement. We both know it has an expiration date." She stepped closer and looked up at me expectantly. "But I understand if you don't want to."

"You're pushing me." Heat and longing filled me. My erection tented my pants, trying desperately to reach out and touch her. "Christ." I let go of her arm and took a step back. "I *am* a breathing, human male. Of course I want to. I just don't think it's a good idea."

"Okay," Blake said simply. She stepped back, dismissed.

"Do you need an ego boost or something?" I asked, annoyed. I wasn't sure what she was playing at, making me ache like this.

She let out a surprised bark of laughter. "No. It's just that I want you to be happy with the arrangement. And I wanted to make it easy for you in case you changed your mind. I didn't want you to be... embarrassed... if you had to make the first move after all your proclamations and decrees against it."

I laughed in spite of myself. "Proclamations and decrees, huh?"

"You *have* been going on about it," Blake said under her breath. "I thought it was like a 'protest too much' kinda thing."

I stopped laughing. My cock was still throbbing, irritated as hell that it wasn't going to get what it wanted. "Don't worry about me. I can take care of myself. And I don't get embarrassed, babe."

"Of course not." It was like a veil was lowered over her face; she seemed to shut down her openness and any honest emotion on cue. "Well, good night. So I'll be seeing you tomorrow?"

"Yes." Disappointment flashed through me as she headed to her room alone, just like I'd instructed. "We have things to do. A wedding to plan. Venues to book. Dresses to buy."

"Dresses? As in my wedding dress?" Blake whirled back toward me, her hair swinging, emitting that scent that made me stiffen even further. *Fuck.* I was going to have to go back to my room and jerk off *again*.

Her eyes were sparkling with excitement, and I

noticed, much to my chagrin, that this pleased me a great deal.

"Yes, Blake. Your wedding dress. I made an appointment with a bridal salon tomorrow. Also, we're having our announcement pictures taken in the Common." I'd had nothing to do with any of this, of course. I'd gotten a lengthy text from Shirley, who'd made all the arrangements and taken care of all the details. She'd only offered to help, but in her typical fashion, she'd gone above and beyond, hiring Boston's best photographer and making an appointment at an exclusive bridal studio on Newbury Street for first thing in the morning.

Blake grinned at me. "Well, I'm looking forward to it. Shopping with you, I mean."

"We'll be having wine at lunch," I assured her. "Shopping drives me to drink."

"Me too." She walked tentatively toward me then leaned up and gave me a quick kiss on the cheek.

"What's that for?" I put my hand over the spot where she'd kissed me, as if I could preserve it. *Jesus, Lucas. Get a fucking grip.*

"For being sweet. And for letting me have a graceful exit after I tried to get you to sleep with me—*again*." Her smile didn't falter.

"My pleasure." I nodded toward her door. "Get some rest. Tomorrow's going to be a long day."

"Yes, sir." She winked at me, and before I could object to her word choice, she disappeared into her room.

With the scent of her hair still all around me, I went as swiftly as I could down the hall to the privacy of my own room so that I could relieve myself.

Again.

BLAKE

I couldn't sleep. Instead, I tossed and turned, finally giving up and staring at the ceiling. *Why am I trying so hard to get Lucas into bed? Is it just because he's handsome and sexy?*

Nah. He was a prime specimen of male physical beauty and power, all muscle and smoldering good looks. But that usually wasn't enough to get me excited. It took a lot more than that.

Not that I was excited. I would never admit to it, anyway.

Is it because he said no?

Maybe. It was certainly a first for me, aside from Vince. Maybe Lucas's rejection stung me more than I cared to admit, and I wanted him to see what he was missing.

But I didn't think that was the real reason.

It's because I like him. I liked Lucas Ford—I liked his brain, I liked his take on the world, and I liked his unflappable confidence. I also liked his green eyes, dimple and big shoulders, but that wasn't the point. I didn't "like" guys. I had sex with them. For money. They were all Johns that way and that was how I preferred it.

So if I slept with him, he would no longer be Mr. Special and I wouldn't be crushed out on him. He would just be a John, like all the rest. And that was what I wanted, for too many reasons to scroll through in my tired head.

Christ. Now I was analyzing myself.

I rolled back over, trying to fall asleep and desperately trying to turn my internal psychoanalyst off.

I did not like her diagnosis *at all.*

LUCAS

I woke up the next morning sporting wood, the kind that wouldn't go down on its own. *Unfreakingbelievable.* I hadn't masturbated this much since I was a high school sophomore. That was right before I smartened up and got a girlfriend—one that was just as horny as me and wasn't interested in talking too much.

Blake's hair spilled out all around her on the bed. I stroked it, my naked body covering hers. My erection rubbed against her wetness. She felt slick beneath me. If I didn't watch it, I was going to come before I even got inside her.

Or got to the best part of the fantasy. I needed to pace myself with Blake, even in my imagination. *For fuck's sake.* I was seriously losing it.

Don't think, don't think, I coached myself, trying to get back to the fantasy. If I didn't get this over with now, I was going to be walking around Newbury Street all day with blue frickin' balls.

Blake arched her back and looked up at me with her wide blue eyes. "I need you," she gasped, sounding as if she would die if I didn't fuck her right now. So I did—I eased my cock into her tight, pink, perfect pussy. Her body clamped around me like a vise.

"Holy fuck, babe," I said as I started to thrust.

"Lucas!" she cried, writhing in pleasure underneath me, her tits bobbing as I fucked her hard. "Oh, fuck!"

"Come for me, baby." I wanted to feel her shatter around me and suck my cock dry already. And this was my *fantasy, dammit.*

"Oh, yes! YES! I fucking love you, Lucas! I love you!"

She fucking *loves* me? What the actual *fuck* was the matter with—

It didn't matter because I came, suddenly and in a

torrent. A soft curse escaped my lips as I exploded, an imaginary Blake still writhing beneath me.

Then there was a knock at my door. "Lucas?"

"What?" I snapped, not thinking. My body still shook with the shock of my orgasm.

"I brought you coffee," a cheery voice called, and then Blake opened the door.

"Can I have some fucking *privacy*?" I roared, my dick still in my hands.

Blake took two steps in, saw me on the bed, opened her mouth—and then it seemed she couldn't manage to close it. "What? Uh, oh boy. Sorry." She looked around in a panic, clutching the mug of coffee she'd brought in. She looked as if she might burst into hysterical laughter or tears. I couldn't tell which.

"Just leave it on the dresser," I said disgustedly, my chest still heaving.

"Okay," she squeaked, setting it down and shooting out of the room faster than Michael Phelps leaving the blocks.

I wiped myself off with a tissue, staring at the ceiling. I was still breathing. My heart was still beating. I was officially living proof that I couldn't die of embarrassment.

As I calmed down, the CEO in me decided to take

charge. I decided that I was going to think of today as a positive challenge.

Or, in an alternative, I was going to need to beat something.

But not my man-meat. That routine was getting retired right now.

FRESH FROM THE SHOWER, where I'd attempted to drown my shame, I sauntered out to the kitchen, mug in hand. I'd decided to just play it cool. Blake was a grown woman; surely she would act like an adult and just let the incident drop.

She was sitting in the living room, reading the newspaper and drinking coffee, a picture of quiet, upscale domestic normalcy. "Hi," she called, not looking at me. "Everything come out all right?" Her shoulders shook in silent laughter.

"Ha ha," I said, but then I gave up and started to laugh, too. "It did, but barely. I'm uh… I'm not used to having company."

Blake nodded, her head still buried in the paper. "I'll remember that. Sorry. I just wanted to give you a coffee. I didn't mean to interrupt your… flow." She started laughing again.

I groaned. "I'm fine, thank you. And I told you—I don't get embarrassed." And yet, my cheeks were flaming.

Blake peered up at me over the paper, taking in my blush. "I know. I remember. That's why this isn't weird, right? It's not weird?"

"I think we've gotten beyond weird." I poured myself another cup of coffee and sat down on a barstool, still watching her. It was actually nice to have her there even though she was currently busting my balls. I never invited the women I slept with to sleep over, let alone hang out in my home.

I love you, Lucas! The image from my earlier fantasy suddenly presented itself to mock me. I shivered, disgusted with myself, and hopped off the barstool. "I'm going to hit the gym before we go out for the day. Please help yourself to some breakfast."

Blake put the paper down and stood up. "Aren't you going to eat?"

"Not now. I'll have a protein shake later."

"Well, can I come with you to the gym?" She suddenly sounded shy, bouncing on the balls of her feet.

"I don't usually have a gym buddy." My tone made it clear that I wasn't keen on the idea.

"You don't have to babysit me. It just gets really boring, sitting around here with nothing to do. Except masturbate." She giggled until she saw the look on my face and abruptly stopped. "You can even pretend you don't know me."

"I might." *Yeah, right.* And let the other guys at The Stratum try to be Blake's gym buddy? *No fucking way.* "Except that's my engagement ring sitting on your finger."

Blake looked down at it and smiled, fingering it. "Right. Except for that." She looked back up at me. "I promise I won't bug you. I can take care of myself. And I won't *ever* make another masturbation joke—I swear."

"Fine." The word escaped before I had the chance to bite it back.

She was ready in five minutes. She wore a plain gray tank top and black running shorts. Her hair was pulled up in a messy ponytail, and she wore no makeup. Yet she still managed to look stunning. She was so pretty in her natural state, it almost hurt to look at her. "Ready?" she asked, all smiles.

I nodded and tried not to stare. She'd already caught me whacking off this morning and had probably guessed that it was her I'd been thinking of. Enough was enough.

Much to my surprise, Blake knew her way around the gym. It almost annoyed me that she never asked me for help or looked my way even once. She ran on the treadmill. She did a weight circuit. She smiled and chatted with every man who spoke to her, but I noticed that she flashed her ring to all of them and mentioned that she was getting ready for her wedding.

I felt wildly, stupidly proud.

"See?" she asked when we got back into the elevator. Her body was glistening with a fine sheen of sweat, which somehow managed to make her look even more attractive. "I didn't bug you once, did I?"

"No," I admitted. For some reason, that really bugged me.

BLAKE

The dresses were absolutely stunning. Mina, the small, elegant woman who was handling our appointment at the Vera Wang Bridal Salon, beamed at me as she showed me the racks. "Wow," was all I could manage to say. We were the only customers in the exclusive shop, which was open by appointment only.

"I agree. They're all wow," she said. "Is there a particular style you're interested in?"

"Honey?" I asked Lucas, who was sitting by the window, tapping furiously into his smartphone.

"Yes, honey?" he asked, never looking up. I was starting to feel as if we were already an old married couple.

"Is there a certain style of dress you like?"

"Nothing poufy," he said, still typing. "I want to see that hot body of yours."

"Men," Mina said, conspiratorially.

"I heard that," Lucas called.

"She kind of has a point, honey," I called back. "But don't mind me; I'm just shopping for a wedding dress. A slutty one."

Lucas finally looked up from his phone. "I didn't say *slutty*, babe." He sounded nagged. "I just don't want your gorgeous figure hidden inside a poufy dress. Is that okay?"

I melted toward him a little, in spite of myself. "Of course, *babe.*" I wanted to wink at him, but I held back.

Mina and I assembled about ten dresses, and she arranged them in a fitting room for me in the back of the store. Lucas stood up, stretched, and started to follow me toward the back.

"What are you doing?" I asked, aghast.

He looked baffled. "Don't you want me to see the dresses?"

"No, I do *not*," I said. "It's bad luck for the groom to see the wedding dress before the ceremony. I got your instructions: no pouf. I'll deliver."

Lucas arched an eyebrow at me. "You're really worried about bad luck?"

I shrugged, trying to play it cool. "I just want everything to be perfect."

"Are you superstitious?" Lucas asked.

"I'm totally superstitious," I admitted.

He put his hand over his heart and grinned at me. "Well, I am humbled that you care enough about our wedding to be superstitious about it."

I grinned back. "Lucas Ford, you have never been humbled a day in your life. Except for maybe this morning." I started giggling. The wedding dresses were so shiny and amazing, I'd almost forgotten about this morning. *Lucas Ford had been whacking off.*

I'd caught a glimpse of him, and I'd been seriously impressed. Which, as one might imagine, wasn't an easy feat for a working girl. I'd thought I'd seen 'em all.

But Lucas had been large. Thick. Hard. Oh, so hard. I'd watched him stroking himself, coming, and I'd been mesmerized.

"Blake." His voice interrupted me. "You promised me you'd drop it about this morning. So stop thinking about my dick and go find a wedding dress."

I felt a blush creep up my neck. "I wasn't *thinking about your dick*." I leaned forward and hiss-whispered at him while Mina fluttered somewhere behind me. "But yes, sir. I'll go find a wedding dress."

He crossed his arms against his massive chest. "I told you to stop calling me 'sir.'"

He sounded as though he was going to come after me, and even though I wouldn't have minded, I hustled to the back to try on the dresses. Mina didn't need to witness our dysfunction, or whatever it was that was growing between us. An unlikely camaraderie. An uneasy alliance. And a growing lust, at least on my part.

Why did I have to see his dick? That was all I was going to be thinking about all day.

But then I went into the dressing room, and Mina handed me the first dress to try on. And like the good blonde that I was, all other thoughts vanished as I inspected the gorgeous dress. I fingered the fine, beaded material and wondered what it would be like to wear something so elegant and shiny on my wedding day.

But it was the third dress I tried on that made my heart stop: I knew it was the one when I saw it.

"That's it! That's the one," Mina said, clapping her hands together, before I'd even said a word.

I beamed at her. "I think so, too! How'd you know?"

She held the bodice of the dress tighter and turned me back toward the mirror. The long gown was covered in intricate lace that shimmered. I had to examine the dress closely to make out all of the ornate details. It was absolutely stunning.

There was a twinkle in Mina's eye. "Same way I know that man out there is the man of your dreams. And that you're the woman of his. Some things are just meant to be."

"Oh. Huh." I smoothed the dress and looked at my reflection in the mirror. "I bet you say that to all the girls," I said playfully, but my heart was suddenly racing.

"No, dear, I don't," she said. "I love it when people get divorced. Repeat business." She swooped my hair over one shoulder and adjusted the dress. "But I don't think you two will be back. Unless you do a vow renewal someday. And I have some *lovely* dresses for that."

"HOLY GUACA-GUACA." Nikki pulled out a long, strapless red gown embellished by a fabric rose. "Isn't this *something*?" She fingered the flower with her fake nails, practically skewering it.

"It's lovely." I swallowed hard. "Could you maybe put it down?"

"Aw, Blakey, stop your worrying." Nikki snapped her gum and tossed her blond curls. "They love us in here."

The fact was Nikki was right. Lucas had arranged for three escorts—Nikki, Helena, and Christie—to meet us at the salon to pick out bridesmaids' dresses. Mina hadn't stopped smiling. Same thing with Lucas, who was tipsy from too much wine at lunch and the attention of excited escort-bridesmaids.

Nikki was the one I'd spent the most time with. She was the closest thing I had to an actual friend. She was short and curvy, with long curly blond hair and pouty lips. Helena was tall and model-thin, with cheekbones that could cut glass. Christie was in the middle height-wise, with what she referred to as an "ample bosom" and wavy chestnut hair. The four of us were considered Elena's top escorts.

"Girls, pick out whatever you like," Lucas had said. They fussed and cooed over him, thanking him profusely and gushing about the store and the upcoming wedding.

Lucas had beamed at them. It'd been a retail roller-coaster ever since.

My coworkers were in the back, trying things on, but they kept catwalking their wares out front for Lucas to admire. Helena—who was six-feet tall with cascading raven hair and an ass you could rest a martini on without spilling it—came out in a skintight, black, strapless bridesmaid dress.

"Very nice," Lucas said, too enthusiastically for my taste. "*Very* nice."

A stab of something utterly foreign pierced me—

jealousy. I glared at him as Helena grinned, tossed her hair over her shoulder, and sashayed back to the dressing room.

He finally noticed my glare. "What?" he asked, flushing.

"This is our *wedding*," I hissed. "Please stop drooling over the bridesmaids."

"I'm not drooling," he said, looking abashed. "I just like that dress."

"Just keep your tongue in your mouth," I snapped. "Drooling in Vera Wang is not acceptable."

"Sheesh," was all he said, but he didn't ogle the other girls.

Finally, dresses were chosen and the fittings were complete. I hugged each of my coworkers, thanking them for agreeing to be part of my big day.

"Are you frickin' kiddin' me?" Nikki asked, popping a fresh piece of gum into her mouth. "We're going to *Vegas.* For your *wedding.* To *him.*" She pointed appreciatively in Lucas's direction. "This is going to be the best weekend *ever*."

"Right?" Lucas asked, his eyes sparkling. I shot him a glare, and he coughed, looking down and inspecting the carpet. I made a mental note not to let him have wine at lunch again.

Everything was happening so fast. The girls all had

airline tickets booked for Friday, so we could meet in Vegas for the rehearsal dinner that night, followed by the ceremony the next day. They were all abuzz with excitement. Even Mina was caught up in it, hugging me and each of my bridesmaids as if we were her new best friends. By the time we left, we'd spent over a hundred thousand dollars on dresses and rush tailoring fees.

I guess we *were* her new best friends.

Exhausted, I practically staggered out of the salon, but Lucas seemed triumphant. He threw his arm around me as we headed down the sidewalk. "I like your friends," he said.

I sniffed. "I noticed."

"Aw, Blakey, don't be sour. It's our *wedding*," he said, teasingly using Nikki's nickname for me. He seemed positively upbeat. "Besides, we have to go home and get dressed up for our engagement pictures. So you need to lighten up."

"Fine," I said. We started through the park, but I was so shopped-out, I was immune to the beauty of the flowering trees and the smiling children riding the swan boats.

"Wait a minute," Lucas said. "I need to talk to some-one." He headed over to a tree that was shading an older man, who was surrounded by bags. "Herman," Lucas said, reaching down and shaking his hand. "It's a beautiful day."

"Always is, big guy," Herman said. "How're you doing?"

Lucas put his arm around me and pulled me against his side. "I couldn't be better. I'm getting married."

"No shit," Herman said. "To her?" He motioned toward me.

"This is Blake Maxwell. Blake, this is Herman Pace. He's an old friend."

"Who're you calling old?" Herman asked. He struggled to his feet and gave me a stately nod. "It's a pleasure, Ms. Maxwell. Congratulations." He looked back and forth between us. "I'm expecting the future holds good things for you two. Both of you with nice smiles like that."

"Thank you," I said, touched.

"We're going out of town for a while," Lucas said. "I'll have Ian come check on you. And here's this." Lucas handed him a card. "Take care."

"Thank you," Herman said. "And congratulations!"

Lucas kept his arm around me and headed toward The Stratum. "Who was that? What did you give him?"

"Herman Pace is a retired air force captain, who now happens to live in the park," Lucas said. "I met him at a function my mother was hosting to raise money for homeless veterans. The man's brilliant."

"So you've... stayed in touch with him?" I asked, surprised by this side of Lucas. "You visit him?"

He shrugged. "I tried to convince him to come work for me, but he likes being retired. Then I tried to buy him a condo, but he prefers the nomadic lifestyle. So I give him gift cards to local restaurants to make sure he eats. In the winter, Ian and I check in and make sure that he goes to the shelter when it's freezing out. Even though he hates to."

I felt touched. "Why do you do that?"

"I like him." Lucas squeezed my hand. "So you see, even though it didn't say so in that *Globe* article, I'm not a completely heartless bastard with the appetite of a zombie. And I can't let my sister have *all* that money. She can afford plenty of oxygen facials with just half. The other half's going to charity, like my mother would have wanted."

"Why didn't she just say that in her will?"

"She wanted to trust us. To act like adults and make the right decision." He checked his watch. "We have to hurry. Are you ready for your close-up?"

I nodded. "I'm ready for anything." That might have been a lie, but the more I got to know Lucas, the more I wanted to believe it was true. For once.

LUCAS

The photography session went well. There was an easy familiarity between me and Blake as we sat in the middle of the park. The photographer had us look into each other's eyes, hold hands, and had me drape my arm over her shoulders. The proofs he sent us afterward looked amazing. We looked like a real-life couple, gorgeous and smiling, all the happiness in the world in front of us.

Looking at the photographs, it was hard to believe it was a lie.

I had dinner delivered to the penthouse that night. We sat outside on the deck, overlooking the park below.

"I'm sorry I gave you a hard time about my friends," Blake said out of the blue. She was trying to get a crouton under the control of her fork and struggling.

"I was being an ass," I said. The other escorts were hot, but salivating over them in front of her had been insensitive.

"You're free to ogle who you like," Blake said, finally skewering the crouton.

I smiled at her. "That's not true. I'm spoken for. Engaged."

"You know what I mean."

I put down my fork. "Blake, I won't be with anyone else while we're together." I hadn't thought this part through, but I meant it. In addition to just being rude, it would be dangerous for me to seek physical release with someone else. If my sister got a hold of something like that, she would be crying fraud immediately.

Blake put down her own fork and raised an eyebrow at me. "You're going to be celibate for a whole year?"

I coughed. When she said it like that... "Aren't you?"

She shrugged. "Yes, but I don't *mind*." Her tone was challenging.

"I don't mind, either."

Blake furrowed her brow as she took a sip of wine. She was obviously mulling something. "Why are you so against... *being* with me? Do I disgust you? I mean—because of what I do?" Her tone wasn't self-deprecating. It was genuinely, intensely curious.

"Listen to me." I reached for her hand and held it across the table. "You are not capable of eliciting disgust from anyone. It doesn't matter what you do. You're a good person, Blakey." I smiled at her, trying to lighten the mood.

She pulled her hand back. "Don't tease me. I'm being serious."

I reached for her again, trapping her hand underneath mine so she couldn't escape. "So am I. You do not disgust me. In fact, the opposite is true. You're gorgeous. I'm attracted to you. I was thinking about you this morning when you so rudely interrupted my jerking off." I felt my heart rate pick up. I was laying it all out for her.

She looked pleased for a moment but then stifled her reaction. "Oh."

"On top of that," I continued, "I think you're a good person. You take care of your mother. You're working as an escort in order to protect the people you love. I *admire* you."

I could feel her knee starting to bounce nervously under the table. "Okay."

"I would sleep with you six ways from Sunday if I thought it wouldn't cause a problem between us down the road. But I think it would. And I can't jeopardize my family fortune in order to test that theory. Okay?"

"Why do you think it would?"

I let out an exasperated groan. "Are you dying to sleep with me? Because you're being awfully stubborn about this."

Blake cleared her throat. "I just want to be sure I understand."

"That's a non-answer, Blakey."

"That's the only answer I've got." Blake smiled at me bravely. "So tell me again."

I drank some more wine and reluctantly let go of her hand. "Ever since Elizabeth and I broke up, I've only had one-night stands with women. I'm sure that sounds terrible."

"*I'm* not going to judge you," Blake said. "Is it because she broke your heart?"

"No." I scrubbed my hand over my face. "I realized that the relationship was a waste of time, and that I didn't want another one. My needs could be met in other, more short-term ways."

"Just sex," Blake offered.

"Right. And after I lived like that for a year or two, I realized I preferred it that way. I didn't have to try to negotiate some messy emotional entanglement. I hadn't met anyone who could hold my interest that long. And that's true for Elizabeth, too. It had just become routine with her. It's not like I was shattered that she married my father. I just thought it was tacky, like everyone else."

"But we won't have a messy emotional entanglement," Blake persisted.

Sheesh. Maybe she really can't stop thinking about my cock.

I smiled smugly to myself. *Wouldn't be the first time.*

"And I'm not saying that because I'm desperate to sleep with you—trust me, I'm not," she said, as though she were reading my thoughts. "*But* I still would like to understand where you're coming from."

"If we have sex, you're going to want it every night," I warned her.

"So *that's* what you're worried about, big boy?"

I shrugged. "I'm just saying."

"I think I've finally met my ego match." Blake laughed then pointed to herself. "You think you wouldn't want *this* every night?"

I chuckled. "Of course I would. Well, maybe I would —or maybe your charms would wear thin when you started snoring next to me. Or maybe you'd turn needy. But that's the problem. You'd be here either way while I figured it out. And if we're married, and we're sharing a bed, and we're having dinner together… for a *year*… that's starting to sound a little bit too much like a relationship to me. And I don't want that. That's messy, and I don't do messy."

"Got it." She drank some more wine. "Enjoy your period of celibacy. I know I will."

"Cheers." I clinked her glass. I sounded sure of myself, but then again, when didn't I?

Later that night, I lay in bed, wide awake. I refused to masturbate. If Blake walked in on me again, she would never let me live it down.

But I was still thinking about her. And not just her

hair and her luscious body. I was thinking about when she'd ordered for me at lunch today, and how we liked the same foods. I was thinking about her cheeks getting heated when I ogled that other escort.

I was thinking about holding her hand and introducing her to Herman Pace. *I'm expecting the future holds good things for you two.* And the pictures, the goddamned engagement pictures…

I lay awake for a long time that night. And I wondered what it would be like if I asked Blake to join me in my bed every night for a year.

And I decided it would be anything but a good thing.

BLAKE

The reservations had been made, the menus chosen, and the bags packed. We knew what we had to do to obtain a valid marriage license as soon as we landed in Las Vegas. I couldn't believe it: we'd planned an out-of-state, black-tie wedding in less than a week.

Having billions of dollars at your disposal sure helped you get shit done.

I decided to call my mother one last time before we left. But it wasn't my mother who answered her cell phone. "Blake?"

"Chelsea?" My stomach plummeted. "Is Mom okay? Is she sick?"

My sister sniffed. "She's fine now that I'm here."

I felt a sudden, intense headache coming on. "What does *that* mean?"

"It means it would've been nice if you'd told me you were going out of town so I could check in on her."

You mean so it was safe for you to come over and ask her for money. I bit the thought back. "She's fine. I've been checking on her. I always do."

My sister snorted. "For a hooker, you sure do have a superiority complex."

I counted backward from ten so I wouldn't jump through the phone and throttle her. "Can I just speak to Mom, please?"

"Fine."

"Hi, honey," my mother said a little too brightly.

"Everything okay?"

"Of course! Your sister and I are just having a nice visit." I could hear the forced cheerfulness in her voice, the way she always sounded when Chelsea came around.

"Okay. I'm leaving town today, so I just wanted to check in. Don't say anything to Chelsea, okay? I'll call you soon."

"Love you, honey," my mom said.

Just as she was hanging up, I heard my sister in the background. "Don't tell Chelsea *what*?" Then the line went dead.

Perfect. Just fucking perfect.

I went and checked my bags one last time. I had some amazing lingerie that Elena had purchased just for this assignment. It was all neatly packed in the side of my suitcase, just in case. Lucas had been very clear that we weren't going to be needing it. As much as I respected his new vow of celibacy, I'd seen the way he'd looked at me. There was a real heat between us, a kind I'd never felt before.

So I decided to pack the lingerie, just in case he changed his mind. I hoped he did. Not only because I wanted to explore that fine body of his, but because I wanted to get him out of my system. I didn't need to be crushed out on my emotionally unavailable billionaire fake fiancé. He seemed like the perfect guy, but I knew the truth: there was no such thing, at least not for me.

The sooner I slept with him, the sooner the version of him I was currently building up in my head would come crashing back to earth. Then we'd both be better off.

Especially me.

Still, I wondered briefly what it would be like for Lucas to hold me. To wake up in his arms, in his bed, every day for a year. I ran my hands over my favorite black lace teddy one final time.

Then I zipped the suitcase shut, fluffed my hair, and

mentally prepared myself for my impending nuptials in Vegas.

LUCAS

"Don't we have to wait in line?" Blake asked, looking curiously around the airport.

"We're flying private."

She just blinked at me. "You own a plane?"

I nodded. "And a helicopter."

"Why do you own a helicopter?" She seemed clearly baffled.

I shrugged.

"You don't know?"

I shrugged again. "I fly it sometimes."

"Lucas Ford, no you do not. All you do is work." Blake crossed her arms over her chest and looked at me skeptically. "When have you flown it?" It didn't sound like a question. It sounded like a taunt.

"Twice."

She raised an eyebrow.

"To my house in Maine."

"And the second time?" she asked.

I coughed. "I flew it back."

"I want you to take me out in it," she said immediately.

"Really?"

She nodded. "I want to go to Maine. And I would like it if my husband flew me there."

A knot of desire, or maybe longing, twisted deep in my chest. *Her husband.* She was talking about me.

Because you paid her, you douche, I reminded myself.

"That's quite the leap of faith. Flying with someone so inexperienced."

She linked her hand through mine and leaned toward me conspiratorially. "It's not much more of a leap than marrying a complete stranger for money. Or agreeing to live with him for a whole year. And *this* seems to be working out all right."

I felt a large, stupid grin spread over my face. "It does, doesn't it?"

"Oh, will you two get a room?" A raucous voice called out from behind us.

I realized that Blake and I were holding hands, staring into each other's eyes. "Brace yourself," I told her.

"For what?"

I groaned. I could practically feel the ground shaking as he approached. "For my college roommate. Jake Ryan."

"The *senator*?" Blake asked, peering over my shoulder.

"The very same," Jake said, coming up and slapping me on the back with his big meat paw of a hand. He was a former college running back who'd recently leveraged his law degree, bigger-than-life personality, and huge physical presence into a seat as a Massachusetts senator.

"Ow," I said, brushing him off. "And *hi*. I wasn't sure if you were going to make it, Mr. VIP. I haven't seen you since Christmas."

Jake scrunched his handsome face into a mask of incredulity. "You think I'd miss your *wedding*? What kind of best friend do you think I am?"

"The kind who's a politician, too busy screwing others and sucking up to remember the little people."

"Can you *please* shut up, little person? And introduce me to this gorgeous, clearly *insane* woman who's agreed to marry you?" He turned to Blake, his eyes sparkling. "Come to Jake and give me a hug, girl! We're practically family now!"

Blake yelped as Jake turned his meat paws loose on her, clamping her and pulling her in for a crushing hug. He kissed the top of her head. "She smells good," he said to me, still holding her.

"I know. Please let go of her."

Jake released her and held her out for his inspection. He let out a low wolf whistle. "*Damn*, Lucas, you finally did something right!"

I karate-chopped his hands from Blake and stepped between them. "Paws off, Jake. And I know—she's fabulous. Now let's get on this plane and start drinking. The whole crew's coming."

Jake looked suddenly wary. "Who do you mean?"

I straightened myself and took Blake's hand protectively. "Serena. My father. Elizabeth. And Blake's bridesmaids."

"Serena? *And* Elizabeth? *Fuck me*," Jake said. His face turned hopeful as he looked at Blake. "Are any of the bridesmaids as hot as you?"

"No," I said quickly. "Besides, they are off-limits to you, Mr. Senator."

Jake turned back to me. "We're going to *Vegas*, dude. Are you going to be a buzzkill this whole trip?"

"Not if you pour me a bourbon before I have to face the firing squad."

Jake nodded solemnly. He understood. He'd known my family for years, and he'd been there for me when my mother died. He'd also been around during the entire shit show that was my father and Elizabeth. "Right. Let's do this. I'm going to need some liquid courage, too. Your sister scares the piss out of me."

We settled in the plane, each with a healthy pour of a drink, and Jake was asking Blake one thousand questions. He did that with new people. Cross-examination was the one thing he'd liked about practicing law. To my amusement, Blake answered his questions flawlessly, charming my burly best friend even as she lied to his face. I would tell him the truth about her and the bridesmaids eventually. But I couldn't risk him melting down in disbelief before my family even boarded the plane.

Which they did, all too soon.

"Keep the drinks coming," I told the flight attendant lowly. "And make sure you hit the three of us first."

"Serena, Elizabeth, Mr. Ford." Jake beamed at them like the master politician he was. "So wonderful to see you!"

"Jake." Serena wiped herself off after he released her from a bear hug. "I was hoping you couldn't make it."

"Aw, Serena, you haven't changed a bit." Jake pinched her cheek until her eyes started to water. "Let's see if we can get you to loosen up a little this weekend, huh? I remember you used to like to party…"

Serena pulled back and gave Jake a filthy look, her face reddening. There had been one night in college that I'd caught the two of them making out. I would encourage Jake to try that again this weekend, but I'd already made other arrangements for my sister.

Just then, the bridesmaids appeared—Nikki, Christie, and Helena. "Yay!" Blake said, popping up. "My girls are here!"

"Blakey!" Nikki pranced over to her and pulled her in for a hug. She was wearing a crop top and what looked suspiciously like a cheerleader skirt. Christie had on the tightest jeans I'd ever seen. Helena wore a skintight dress and spiked high heels.

"This is *awesome*," Jake said, staring at Blake's friends. My father looked positively gleeful, too. *Christ.*

"Don't touch them," I warned Jake. "I'll explain later."

"You've gotta be fucking kidding me, dude." He spoke low enough that my family couldn't hear.

"I'm not kidding," I said. "The buzzkill continues."

Serena was aghast as she watched Blake and the bridesmaids. "Who are *they*?"

I smiled, suddenly feeling excited. "Blake's friends. Her bridesmaids."

"They must work in *marketing*." According to my sister's tone, marketing was a seriously filthy business.

I nodded. "Yeah, I think they do."

My sister grabbed the flight attendant as she passed. "I need another drink. Make it a double."

"Me too," said Jake, checking out Nikki and her cheerleader skirt with longing.

"Me too," I said. I watched the spectacle and rubbed my hands together with glee. I was probably going to enjoy this weekend more than I should.

BLAKE

We were all staying at The Warner, which was arguably Vegas's most upscale hotel. The wedding was scheduled in one of its private courtyards for six o'clock the following evening. I practically staggered through the lobby, awed by the opulence that surrounded me. I'd never been to Vegas before, and I was completely unprepared for the spectacle.

The hotel was enormous, with soaring ceilings and chandeliers. And there were colorfully decorated trees inside. "Those are real trees," I whispered to Nikki as we traipsed through the lobby.

"I know, right? Vegas is the coolest. It's like Disneyworld for adults!" She adjusted her crop top and looked around. "What're we doing tonight?"

"Huh?" I was still gawking at the trees and all the pretty, twinkling lights.

Nikki twisted her ponytail around her finger and smiled at me indulgently. "I asked you what we were doing tonight. But what I *should* have said is that I'm really happy for you. Lucas is gorgeous." She looked around then conspiratorially leaned toward me. "And he actually seems *nice*."

That pulled me from my reverie. "He's very nice." I smiled at my friend. "And we're having dinner tonight, all of us, at some steak house. I think it's pretty formal." I eyed her cheerleader skirt.

She smoothed it and winked at me. "I got the message, your highness. I'll clean myself up. Elena made me promise to be on my best behavior."

"And I'm sure you will be."

"What about… them?" She jerked her head in the direction of Elizabeth, Franklin, and Serena Ford. They were speaking pointedly to a concierge, seemingly oblivious to the impressive lobby.

"They're never on their best behavior as far as I can tell. We need to get them drunk and keep them drunk all weekend so they're at least tolerable. Okay? And don't let the dad hit on you. I don't want to start trouble with his wife."

"What about the senator?" Nikki asked nonchalantly.

"I think he's off-limits too, sweetie. Sorry." I patted her arm. "But we'll still have fun, okay?"

Nikki nodded. "Sure. I'm gonna go hang out by the pool for a while first."

"Okay. Thank you for being here." I gave her a hug.

"Aw, Blakey. I wouldn't miss this for the world. And I promise I'll be on my best behavior." Nikki sashayed off, probably to put on the world's smallest bikini and have margaritas by the pool.

I was still worried about what she was going to wear to dinner.

Lucas finished speaking with the concierge and headed toward me. He looked so handsome, wearing dark-rinsed jeans and a white button-down shirt. My pulse quickened as he approached. *Easy, girl,* I warned myself. I, too, needed to be on my best behavior this weekend.

He took my hand. "Let's go."

"What about the others? Jake?" I asked.

"They're fine. Jake especially." He hit the button for the top floor of the hotel, and I held my breath as we went up. What we were about to do was sinking in and it was starting to feel surreal. I was getting married to the billionaire next to me tomorrow night. *Nothing to worry about.* I was just going to be married, for money, in front of one hundred guests, a justice of the peace, and God himself.

"Are you okay?" Lucas asked. "You look a little pale."

"I think I need to eat something. Too many cocktails on the plane."

"Right." He whipped out his phone and tapped something furiously into it. The elevator slowed, and he looked up. "This is us." He pulled me through the door as soon as it opened.

As far as I could see, there was only one door on this level. Lucas pressed his thumb against a scanner, and a moment later, the door swung open.

"They have your thumbprint?" I asked, completely baffled.

"Pretty cool, huh?"

"Yeah. And *whoa,*" I said, looking around as we walked into the suite. The room was stunning, like nothing I'd ever seen. We entered at the top of a sweeping, curved staircase. The room below was enormous and sumptuous, with a wall of windows several stories high. The marble floors sparkled in the natural light.

Lucas held out his hand to me and grinned, clearly pleased with my reaction. "My lady."

I took his hand and followed his lead down the stately staircase. When we reached the living room below, I noticed several things all at once. A fire roared in the fireplace, with multiple couches tastefully arranged around it; there was an enormous dining room with a dark, sleek table that sat twelve; pictures that looked very much like original artwork hung on the walls; and what appeared to be a private pool stretched the length of the outside patio.

I stepped closer to the windows, enthralled by the amazing view of the city, spread out in every direction. "This is our… *room*?" I could have fit five of my Southie apartments in this place.

"It's our suite." Lucas flopped down on one of the couches and checked his phone. "Hold on a minute. The butler's here. He needs to come in through the servant's entrance." He got up and headed toward the dining room.

"*Servant's* entrance?" I called after him, utterly agog.

"Yes, set it on the table," I heard him instruct. Suddenly, the man I assumed was our butler came into view along with two waiters. They set the dining room table with candles, water, wine, and plates heaped with food. Then they bowed to Lucas and headed swiftly back to their own entrance, wherever the hell that was.

I pushed my awe to the side as soon as the smell hit me. *Yum.* I hustled to the table and sat down eagerly, ogling the food. There was miso soup, vegetarian sushi, and pad thai with chicken. "How did you know I loved this sort of food?"

A small smile played on Lucas's lips as he watched me start to eat. "You have good taste. It was a logical assumption."

The soup warmed me, making my whole body relax. "I'm so hungry, I'm being rude. Please, sit and join me." I calmed down as I continued to eat. Vegas had already shocked and awed me, and we'd only just checked in.

"My pleasure." Lucas sat down. "We'll go apply for the marriage license after this. We have to go to the county clerk's office."

"I know." I nodded. "We need to present our identification, and then the clerk can issue the license." I'd done my research. I didn't want to come all this way and have technical difficulties derail our plans.

"Perfect," Lucas said. "And then we have a dinner reservation at nine. That should be... interesting."

"With four escorts and your family?" I arched an eyebrow at him. "That might be the understatement of the year."

LUCAS

"The trick is," Nikki said, fanning herself, "to put the

lime in your mouth before you've even swallowed. That makes the whole thing go down so much easier."

"How many of these have you *done*?" I asked. The world seemed to tilt as I examined the neat row of tequila shots lined up on the oak bar.

"Tonight? I dunno." Nikki shrugged and handed me another shot. "Don't worry about me. I do this all the time. This is like a Wednesday night in Southie for me, not a Friday night in Vegas. This"—she motioned to our party, a large part of whom were already intoxicated and showing it—"is strictly amateur night."

"You sure make it look easy." Jake squinted at Nikki suspiciously. "But I feel like I'm gonna puke already." I'd been keeping an eye on my friend as he'd had several bourbons on the plane, followed by a bottle of wine at dinner, then three tequila shots with Nikki. Former linebacker or not, he was starting to look a little green.

"See?" Nikki turned to me, jerking her thumb at Jake and clinking her glass to mine conspiratorially. "Amateur night."

"I'm not a freaking amateur," Jake said. He grabbed a shot off the bar and regarded it. "Let's do this. I'm a lot of things, but I'm no pussy."

Nikki downed her shot, raised an eyebrow at him, and placed the empty glass on the bar. "We'll see, big guy."

I finished off my shot then tapped Nikki on the shoulder. "You can't sleep with him. Stop flirting."

Her lip curled up. "I'm not flirting with *him*. He's a *Democrat,* for Christ's sake."

Jake's face turned stormy. "I'm from Massachusetts. Everybody from Massachusetts is a Democrat."

"Not me," Nikki said. "I'm a Libertarian. Now all we need's a decent candidate..."

Jake and Nikki looked ready to spar, but I held up my hand to stop them. My tongue felt thick and I was worried I wouldn't be able to get the words out. "Don't even hate fuck him, okay?" I begged Nikki. "I'll s'plain later."

Nikki nodded and knocked back another shot. "Got it, boss."

I scrunched my eyes up at her. "Did Blake tell you to call me that?"

"No." Nikki adjusted her dress and looked at me as if I were crazy.

"Where is she, anyway?" I turned around and looked through the bar with squinted eyes. That had been my seventh shot. Plus, all the wine I'd guzzled at dinner sitting across from my father, trying to numb my brain. I should have known better, but damn, I couldn't let Nikki drink me under the table.

But she was sitting upright, and I was squinting. Epic fail.

I saw Blake still sitting at the table with Serena, engrossed in a conversation about God only knew what.

"She's with your sister—oh, fuck," Jake said. "You better go get her. Rescue her and shit." His voice sounded slurry, but maybe my ears were just fuzzy.

"Okay." I stood up, not at all steadily. "Remember, I'm bunking with you tonight." I patted Jake on the chest.

"Right, right," he said, but I could tell I'd already lost his attention to Nikki. I headed over toward Blake and my sister. "Blakey," I interrupted, "can I talk to you?"

"Blakey?" Serena asked. The two bottles of wine she'd polished off at dinner had done nothing to help her attitude. "Seriously?"

"Seriously," I said. It came out *srlsy.*

My sister furrowed her brow and watched as Blake stood up and walked me out of Serena's earshot, wrapping her arms around me to offer support.

"Did you do shots with Nikki? A lot of them?" she asked, clearly concerned as she struggled underneath my weight.

I nodded at her. I didn't want to seem like I couldn't carry my liquor, or worse, tell her I liked her.

"You need to go to bed." She turned back to Serena. "Will you excuse me? He clearly needs help."

Serena nodded. "You're a better woman than I am." She looked at me with thinly veiled disgust.

"Damn right," I said.

"Lucas, stop." Blake looked at Serena apologetically. "See you tomorrow."

My sister shocked me by giving Blake a sympathetic smile. "Good luck with him. You're going to need it. I'm gonna go get hammered. My family's driving me to drink, as usual."

"Were you two being *friendly*?" I watched as Serena made a beeline for the bartender. "What the hell were you talking about?"

"I'll tell you when you can think straight." Blake herded me toward the elevator.

"Twentieth floor," I croaked.

"We're on the top floor, babe," she reminded me gently.

"Not me. I'm sleeping with Jake tonight." I slumped against the cool wall of the elevator, relishing the smooth feeling against my hot skin.

"Why? We have more than one bedroom. Plus, I don't think you should be too worried about breaking your celibacy vow tonight," she said, eyeing me.

"But it's tradition," I insisted. "The bride and groom have to sleep apart."

"You're exaggerating the rule—they're just not supposed to see each other before the ceremony." Blake sighed. "Plus, I need your thumbprint to get into the room."

I shoved my phone at her. "Text Jake. Make him come get me."

Blake groaned. "He looked like he was more interested in getting Nikki."

"Just do it," I begged.

"Fine." She grabbed my phone, texted quickly, then hauled me out of the elevator. She took my thumb and pressed it against the scanner. The door swung open, and Blake eyed the winding staircase. "Ugh..."

"I can do it." At this point, I was pretty sure that it was my words that were fuzzy rather than my ears.

"Put your arm around me," Blake snapped. We hobbled down the stairs, and she deposited me, somewhat abruptly, on one of the couches. She hustled off and came back with a glass of water and two pills. "Ibuprofen," she explained. "Take them before you die, or wish you had."

I swallowed the pills and looked up at her. She was a little blurry. "Does my sister *like* you?" I asked.

"No. I mean, she likes me more than she likes *you*, but that's not really saying anything." Blake flopped down across from me. "She wanted to talk about Robert. She was just drunk. And lonely. Weddings can be hard for people."

I perked up. "Thass good. I'm gonna take care of that."

"What do you mean? Oh, never mind. Just lie back and close your eyes. You look like you're going to fall over." She came over and adjusted me, putting a pillow behind my head. "Amateur," she said under her breath.

"I heard that."

"Good," Blake said. "I can't believe you let Nikki drink you under the table. She's never going to let you live this down."

"I'll show her."

Blake laughed. "Oh yeah, big guy. You really look like it right now."

I opened one eye and peered at her. "This is the most fun I've had in a long time."

She nodded. "Me too." She was still blurry, but I thought she looked suddenly solemn.

I tried to reach for her, but my arm didn't want to move. "So why do you look so sad?"

"I'm not. I'm thoughtful. I'm thinking about what my life is going to be like at this time next year."

"Don't think about that." I closed my eyes. "I don't want to think about it, either. I like you, Blakey. I like having you around."

"You flatter me."

"S'the truth." *A drunken man's words are a sober man's thoughts.* "I like you, and I don't like anyone."

My phone beeped. Blake grabbed it then went up the stairs. A moment later, someone whistled. "Nice place —*very* nice," Jake's voice boomed. "How you doin', soldier? Not so good?" he called down to me.

"Shut up," I croaked. The words barely got out.

"Don't worry. I got him." Jake rumbled down the stairs. He hoisted me up, ignoring my groaning protest. "He said it was important that he let you have some alone time until the ceremony," he told Blake. "No matter how drunk he is, I know he'd want to respect that."

"Thank you," I said. My voice came out muffled against Jake's chest.

"Thanks, Jake," Blake said. "And you." She leaned over and kissed me gently on the cheek. "Good night."

"I like you, babe. I really like you." I reached for her, my voice still muffled. "I can't wait until tomorrow."

"Get some rest and sober up." She sounded tired.

It was only later, when I was attempting to sleep on Jake's couch as he snored heavily nearby, that I realized she hadn't said she liked me back.

I HURT bad the next morning, but not as badly as I should have. I sent out a silent prayer of thanks to Blake for providing me with painkillers before I passed out. Then I just lay there until Jake stopped snoring, got up, and made us coffee.

When I ventured sitting up, my head felt as if there were rocks rolling around inside it. Mean rocks.

I sat down heavily next to Jake on the deck with my coffee. "So, quick question for you," he said.

I rubbed grit from my eyes. "Yes?"

"Last night, when we were leaving your room, you told Blake you liked her." Jake squinted at me, and I noticed how bloodshot his own eyes were.

"So?"

"So why didn't you tell her you *loved* her?" My friend looked stymied. "You *are* marrying her this afternoon and all."

I coughed. "Oh. That."

Jake took a sip of his coffee. "Just tell me the truth. Don't make me interrogate you. I have a bitch of a headache."

I sighed and leaned back against the chair. "I hired her to marry me. She's an escort."

"I knew it!" Jake hopped up and started pacing. Then he winced as if moving hurt and quickly sat back down. "Well, actually, I didn't think Blake was. I thought her friends were, though. Never met a woman who could out-drink me like that. Nikki didn't even wobble when she got up. I knew she was a professional *something*."

"Which is why I told you to stay away from her. You're a senator now. That's a scandal you don't need."

Jake shrugged. "She's cute, though."

"Stop. You *can't*. And you have to pretend you don't know. You can't let my sister figure it out, or she'll go nuts and this whole thing will blow up."

"Don't worry about it. I work in Washington now. I've got lying down to a science." He sat back down and looked at me. "I thought you and Blake were the real deal, though. I saw the way you were looking at her."

"I like her—just like I said. But there's nothing going on with us. We're getting married, and then she has to live with me for a year so I can inherit my share of the trust."

Jake laughed. "You're getting married, you're living together for a year, but there's 'nothing going on' with you two." He made air quotes in what I believed was an effort to truly annoy me. "That's classic Lucas Ford, right there. My man of steel. Nothing gets to you."

"It's a business arrangement," I explained with growing annoyance. "I'm not even sleeping with her."

Jake looked stunned. "Are you fucking kidding me? She's *gorgeous*. And she's an *escort*."

"I know."

"So what's your problem?" He sounded dumbfounded.

"I don't have a problem." I tried to keep my voice even. "And I don't want any. That's why we're not sleeping together."

"You worried about her getting pregnant?"

"No. Jesus." The thought hadn't even crossed my mind.

"You worried you're not man enough?"

My temples were starting to pound. "Shut up, Jake."

"Or are you worried that you might like her too much?" Jake sounded smug.

Herein lied the problem with spending time with my best friend. He knew me too well. I should have been at my office, where everyone was too afraid to talk to me—and I could fire anyone who tried. "You're making my hangover worse."

"One thing I will tell you—practically the only thing I remember from law school," Jake said.

That got my attention. "What?"

Jake grinned at me. "You have to sleep with her to consummate the marriage. Otherwise, it can be annulled. Or contested. If Serena's trying to prove it's a fraud, that's an angle she could work."

"How would she go about that?" I asked. "How would she ever know?"

"No idea, bro. But you know your sister. She's crazy enough to try it. So you better fuck your wife tonight." He put his hands behind his head, smiling and looking satisfied with himself.

"What?" I snapped. "What are you smiling about?"

"Lucas likes Blake, Lucas like Blake," he chanted then expertly maneuvered out of the way of my fist when I tried to punch him.

"Fuck you," I muttered.

Jake laughed. "Best. Weekend. Ever."

BLAKE

"You look gorgeous, honey," Helena said. She dabbed her eyes with a tissue. "Like an angel."

"Thank you." I faced myself in the mirror as the makeup artist put the final touches on my lipstick. "She's doing a great job with the makeup. That helps."

Both Helena and the makeup artist snorted. "You look gorgeous because you're gorgeous," Christie said, coming to stand next to me.

"That's the truth," the makeup artist said. "I don't think I've ever seen a more beautiful bride."

"Oh, that's nice. You guys are making me feel good, which is helping with my nerves." My nerves were, in fact, getting the better of me. I was excited to put on the dress, but I felt silly about it. What was I really excited about? This wedding would be legal, but it wasn't real. Lucas was going to be my husband on paper, in name only. So why did I have butterflies?

I heard some commotion from the back of the dressing room. "What's going on?" I asked Christie.

She grimaced a little. "I don't think Nikki's feeling too good."

"That's just great." Still, I laughed a little. Nikki always liked to talk tough, so it was amusing that the tequila had finally caught up with her last night. A moment later, she stumbled toward me, adjusting her long, strapless bridesmaid gown.

"Oh, Blakey, you look beautiful." Her eyes shimmered with tears. "I can't wait to see you walk down that aisle."

"Are you sure you're up for this?" I asked skeptically. She looked beautiful as always, but she also looked a little pale.

Nikki straightened her shoulders. "I'm fine, and I wouldn't miss this for the world. Now just excuse me while I go throw up."

"Amateur," I called as she hustled to the bathroom.

"I heard that!" Nikki slammed the door behind her.

The makeup artist put a tiny bit of lip gloss onto my lips. "I think you're ready," she said kindly.

I nodded and stood up a little shakily. "As ready as I'll ever be."

More people were seated in the pews than I was expecting. I stood at the end of the aisle, just out of sight, and felt myself sway a little.

"Easy, girl," Jake said softly, coming up beside me. He linked his arm through mine. "I've got you. It's my job to walk you down the aisle. But first, Lucas wanted me to give you a couple of things." He motioned to the wedding planner. "I need Blake for a minute. In private."

"She needs to be coming down the aisle in five minutes," the wedding planner said, adjusting her headset. "But you can use the antechamber until then so you can have a little privacy."

Crisply efficient, she led us to a small room and closed the door behind us. I turned to Jake in a panic. "Is he having second thoughts?"

Jake let out a bark of laughter. "You should be so lucky. He just wanted to give you a few things before the ceremony." Jake took out a box and opened it; inside were five different items. He pulled out the first one, a beautiful gold bangle. "This is something old," he explained as he slipped the bracelet onto my wrist. "It was Lucas's mother's."

Next, he pulled out a bobby pin. "Can you put this in

your hair?" he asked hopefully. "This is your something new, but I have no idea what to do with it."

I smiled and took it from him, securing it into my hair.

"Here's your something borrowed." Jake smiled as he handed me a shiny penny. "It's my lucky penny. Lucas borrowed it from me to give to you."

I took the lucky penny, air-kissed it, and tucked it safely inside my bra.

"I won't tell Lucas I saw you do that," Jake said, chuckling. "And here's the last thing. Your something blue." He handed me a lacy blue garter, looking sheepish, and shrugged. "Lucas is more traditional than you might think."

I beamed at him. "He knows I'm superstitious." I slid the garter up on my thigh, carefully navigating my beaded dress.

"Yeah, he did mention that." Jake held out his arm for me. "You think you're ready for this?"

"There are a lot of people out there," I said nervously. I fingered the bracelet that Lucas had sent to me. "But I feel better about it now."

Jake gave me a quick look. "I'm only gonna say this to you once because Lucas would punch me. But he is *definitely* into you."

I felt myself blush a little. "That's sweet, Jake, but you don't know the whole story about us—"

"I do," Jake said, interrupting me. "Why else would I be trying to convince you that he likes you right before you marry him?"

I shrugged. My nerves really started to thrum.

"Just give him a chance. That's all I'm asking."

I nodded solemnly. "I can do that." I wasn't sure if I was lying to Jake or lying to myself with that answer.

But as we started down the aisle, I had a feeling I was about to find out.

LUCAS

It was just me and the bridesmaids waiting up front. I nodded solemnly at several of the guests: my cousin James and his wife, Audrey; Shirley, my assistant, and her husband; and several other relatives that I hadn't seen in a very long time.

Serena's ex-husband, Robert, was there, as was our trust administrator. I'd invited them both out of spite. Serena had looked as though she were about to pass out when she saw Robert, but he only looked tense and a little sad. I reminded myself to speak to him after the ceremony and thank him for coming. We used to be friends, and I hadn't seen him in a long time.

I was surprised at how many people had shown up on such short notice. I guessed their curiosity had gotten the better of them. Lucas Ford, ruthless loner billionaire, was finally tying the knot. I'd tried to avoid making eye contact with James and Audrey after we'd said our initial hellos. They knew the truth, and I didn't want to see the curiosity burning in their eyes. Everyone there was curious, but not for the same reason as my cousin and his ex-escort wife.

We were in a special outdoor section of The Warner—a beautiful, ethereal garden filled with twinkling white lights and flowers. Blake had chosen well. Even though we were in Vegas, the setting was classical, almost magic.

I felt excited, which annoyed me.

But all thought, rational and otherwise, ceased when the wedding march started and I saw Blake. She was standing at the top of the aisle, holding onto Jake for dear life. She looked magnificent in her wedding dress. I couldn't breathe, let alone think. Her long white gown fit her graceful figure like a glove. I could see every curve of her beautiful body, but the dress was so much more than just that. She was absolutely stunning in it. Her long blond hair was loose around her shoulders, and I saw my mother's bracelet sparkling on her wrist. When our eyes locked and she smiled at me, my heart stopped.

I briefly noticed my sister, who was looking at me with her brow furrowed, as if she couldn't piece something together. But I couldn't concentrate on anyone but Blake. She seemed to glide toward me, that same happy smile on her face as she looked at each of her bridesmaids. Jake was beaming the whole way down the aisle. I knew what he was thinking: that he was delivering the goods. I pushed my annoyance with him to the side. I was about to get married to the most beautiful woman in the world.

And I was a hell of a lot more excited than I should have been.

Blake finally reached me and handed her bouquet to Nikki, who was her maid of honor. Then she turned and grabbed my hands, holding on tight.

"Hi," I said stupidly.

"Hi." Blake's smile was infectious. "Thank you for the gifts. They mean a lot."

"I know you're superstitious. And I wanted you to have my mother's bracelet."

"I'm touched. Truly," she said softly, squeezing my hands.

The justice of the peace came out, and everyone went quiet.

"Dearly beloved, we are gathered here today to witness the union of Blake Maxwell and Lucas Ford—"

Nikki suddenly turned and ran for the bushes behind the altar. She threw up noisily onto one of them. Everyone in the audience groaned.

"Amateur," Jake called, laughing.

She served him with a quick, fierce glare, wiped her mouth, looked at Blake apologetically, then grabbed the bouquets she'd dropped on the ground. "Well, go *on*," she said to the officiant.

He smiled at her with good humor, his eyes sparkling. "It's Vegas," he said to the crowd, shrugging. There were chuckles as Nikki took a brief, red-faced bow. "Now, let's try this again."

Blake and I each listened to the officiant and repeated our vows solemnly, our hands remaining clasped. I didn't take my eyes off of her once. She smiled the whole time, giving me strength and courage to recite the words in front of all of our guests. Then, finally, it was over.

"I now pronounce you husband and wife," the officiant said, beaming. "You may now kiss the bride."

I wrapped my arms around Blake, careful of her dress,

and pulled her to me. I put my lips against hers gently, but then she threw her arms around my neck and deepened the kiss. The crowd whooped and hollered as our kiss lingered. Blake's hands twined through the hair at the base of my neck. My whole body was on fire for her. I finally pulled back, embarrassed, but she had that same smile on her face. She laced her fingers through mine, and we turned to face our guests together, triumphantly, as husband and wife.

"ROBERT. So glad you could make it." I clapped my ex-brother-in-law on the back. He stood there stiffly. I pulled back and noticed that he had dark circles underneath his eyes. "How've you been?"

"Busy." He nodded. "Exhausted." He was an emergency room physician at Boston Medical, one of the biggest inner-city hospitals. "Congratulations, by the way. I never thought I'd see the day."

"Me either. But Blake's special."

"I'll say. She's even gotten Serena to behave somewhat." We watched as my new wife and his ex briefly chatted about something. Serena actually laughed. Robert turned back to me. "Why did you invite me to your wedding?"

I leveled him with a stare. "Why did you come?"

He turned back toward my sister. "I think you know why."

I clapped him on the shoulder. "Go have a drink with her. You know she's nicer when she's wasted."

Robert scrubbed a hand across his face. "Not always." But he headed toward my sister nonetheless. Blake looked up at me then and smiled, making my heart seize. My stupid fucking heart couldn't seem to get this straight. It was a pity that I couldn't fire both it and my cock. They were both giving me a hell of a time.

Wine? Please? Blake mouthed, and I nodded, heading to the bar.

"Not only are you an amateur, you're a libertarian," Jake was telling Nikki. "And I can't believe you didn't vote for me. Frankly, I'm disappointed in you."

Nikki was nursing a ginger ale. "No one's more disappointed than I am," I heard her say. "About the puking. Not about the voting. I'm not sorry about that one bit."

"You should be ashamed about both." Jake's voice was stubborn.

"I'll still drink you under the table—I'm ready to prove that right now," Nikki said. "Hair of the dog. Let's get some shots going, Senator. I believe you're all talk—all you Democrats are."

"Bring it on," Jake said. He nodded at the bartender.

"Start lining up the tequila shots. I have a Libertarian I need to school."

Nikki tossed her hair. "We'll see."

"We all saw you and that bush," Jake taunted.

"Do you have to keep bringing that up?"

I chuckled as I watched them, then I signaled to the bartender for two glasses of wine. Blake and I had both been taking it easy on the alcohol, but we were still sharing toasts with our guests. Surprisingly, the wedding reception was fun. Being in Vegas had put everyone in a celebratory mood. But now that we'd been drinking for several hours straight, things were starting to get out of hand. Helena and one of my cousins were dirty dancing. It was starting to look like a public sex act. My father and Elizabeth were on the dance floor, glued to each other, whispering and looking as if they might need a contraceptive device. Serena and Robert were now in a secluded corner, having what looked like a heated argument.

Rupert, the administrator of my family trust, approached the bar with a stagger. He'd been my mother's trust attorney and a valued confidant for years before she died. Of course, that wasn't the reason I'd asked him to join us.

"Lucas, my boy! Congratulations." He grasped my

hand lightly and shook it. "You two make a fine couple. I know your mother would be proud."

"Thank you, Rupert. I invited you to honor her memory."

Rupert looked at me skeptically. "Let's be honest. You wanted to nip Serena's impending fraud campaign in the bud." He was slightly unsteady on his feet, looking as though he'd had a few.

I smiled at him. "I wanted to get out in front of it. Yes."

He slapped me on the arm. "You don't need to worry." He eyed Blake appreciatively across the room. "Everything looks good to me. Your mother would be happy to see you settled."

I clinked my glass against his. "Cheers to that." He staggered back to the bar, and I headed toward Blake. "I think we should get going soon. This is starting to get messy, and you know how I feel about messy."

Blake rolled her eyes good-naturedly. She hadn't stopped smiling all night. "Oh yeah. I know all about that."

I leaned closer so I could whisper in her ear. "I think we should have a brief round of PDA if that's okay with you. The trust administrator's here." Rupert seemed perfectly satisfied with the marriage, but I wanted to be sure. And also, I wanted...

I ran my hands down her arms. Blake's skin felt hot to my touch as she gazed up at me, her lips parted. My cock jumped to attention, and I leaned down, grazing my lips against hers. I put my hand on her back and felt her arch. *You need to consummate the marriage.* Jake's voice rang in my head.

I crushed my lips against hers, and she pressed against me, her tongue meeting and tangling with mine. I pulled back slightly, and she let out a low moan. I dug my fingers into her hair and kissed her again until I heard a loud wolf whistle and applause all around us. We pulled apart, embarrassed, and found that we were surrounded by our guests, who were whooping and hollering. I saw Shirley wiping her eyes, my cousin Shane with his face buried in Helena's chest, and Serena with her arms crossed, glaring at me.

"I think we should go. But there's someone we need to speak to first." I grabbed her hand and maneuvered her over to where James and Audrey were slow dancing with their arms wrapped around each other. "I hate to interrupt, cousin—"

James straightened up and released his wife immediately. "But you're narcissistic, and you always come first." James grinned at me and shook my hand. "Congratulations, Lucas. Blake. That was a lovely ceremony, aside from the vomiting."

"Oh, honey, stop." Audrey stepped forward and kissed Blake on both cheeks. "It's a pleasure to meet you! Congratulations on your marriage." She turned to me, her brown eyes gleaming. "It's nice to see you looking so settled, Lucas."

"I'm full of surprises," I said. "It was nice of you guys to come. Where are the kids?"

James pulled Audrey back to him and wrapped his arms possessively around her. The way they touched made me want to reach out and grab Blake, which I did.

"With their nanny," James said. "We're flying out first thing in the morning. So we're going to make the most of tonight, right, babe?" He nuzzled Audrey's neck.

Audrey swatted him, but her eyes were sparkling. "Right, babe." She turned her attention back to us. "We really are thrilled for you two. Blake, if you ever want to talk about anything, call me. I'd love to get to know you better."

"Thank you," Blake said, clearly touched. But Audrey had already turned back to her husband, who wrapped his arms firmly around his wife.

James looked up at me one last time. "Call me," he commanded. "And come out to California to meet my kids, dammit."

"How many do you have, again?" I asked. James looked as though he was going to come after me, but I started laughing. "Just kidding. Blake and I will come out."

"Good," James said. "Now please leave us alone. This is date night."

"I think we need to be alone, too." I grabbed Blake's hand and pulled her toward the elevator, making sure no one was watching us make our exit. I wanted to escape the crowd and be alone with her, and I didn't want any more cheering.

"Yes, sir." Blake beamed. "Or should I just start calling you husband?" She drank some more wine, and I could tell that she was a little tipsy.

"How about I call you Mrs. Ford, and you can call me Mr. Ford?"

"It's impersonal. Therefore, I like it." Blake drained her glass as the elevator doors closed.

I pressed against her. "I'm curious to find out what else you like."

She tossed her hair and looked up at me, a challenge in her eyes. "Is that so?"

"It is if I say so." I pressed my lips to hers.

BLAKE

Maybe it was the wine, but when he kissed me, something inside me loosened a little. And then I felt as if I were going to burst.

I opened my mouth for his, relishing the feel of his tongue as it tentatively explored my mouth. He was more languorous now that we were away from the crowd, taking his time, making my body light up as if I were being consumed by a fever. When our tongues connected, a jolt of electricity went through my body, all the way down to the ache in between my legs. "I want you," I said against his mouth. I stopped myself abruptly and pulled back. "I'm sorry. I know we talked about this—"

Lucas kept his hands on me. "Stop, Mrs. Ford. I'm the

one who kissed you, remember? I want to do this. Besides… we have to."

I pulled further away from him. "What do you mean, we *have* to?"

He adjusted his tux, his face turning serious. "Jake used to be a lawyer. I told him the truth about us. I hope you don't mind, but he guessed that there was something funny going on, anyway."

"I don't mind. Jake seems like a good guy. But what were you saying—about him being a lawyer?" My head, which had been fuzzy with lust and champagne, was clearing fast.

Lucas shrugged, looking sheepish. "He told me that our marriage wouldn't be considered legally valid if we didn't consummate it."

"So are you only kissing me because you have to?"

"Yes." He looked at the ceiling then looked at the floor, the color in his cheeks rising. "No." Lucas seemed abashed, but this was music to my ears. We were really going to do this, and it was for business reasons. No strings. No ties. No crushes. But I got to be with him. And I wanted that… even if I could barely stand to admit it to myself.

"Well then, I understand." I kept my voice even and professional. "And if you're asking me if that's acceptable, well… I accept. Let's consummate this thing."

A cloud passed over Lucas's handsome features but disappeared quickly. He smiled at me. "I've never thought of 'consummate' as a sexy word, but when you put it that way? I like it. I like it a lot, Mrs. Ford."

Excitement rushed through me as I trailed my fingers down his tuxedo. I felt as if I were about to open the shiny Christmas present I'd been hoping for all year. His piercing green eyes became hooded. He ran his fingers through my hair, twisting it and greedily pulling me closer.

The elevator stopped at our floor, and the door opened. He reached for my hands. "Come on, Blakey." I tilted my head at him, questioningly. "That's still my favorite nickname for you. Even over Mrs. Ford," he explained. And then, ever thoughtful, he picked me up and carried me over the threshold of our honeymoon suite.

He kept his eyes locked with mine as he carefully carried me down the stairs and through the suite. Lucas placed me gently on my feet just inside the enormous bedroom. I looked up at him and threw my arms around his neck, thrilling at the feel of him, loving that his gorgeous face was so close to mine. I drank in all the details—his dark curls, his dimple, his green eyes.

"Tell me that you want to do this." He ran his hands down my back.

"I want to do this," I said eagerly. "I want to do this *now*." I leaned up and kissed him, hard. He crushed his lips to mine, and our tongues found each other again. He pressed the small of my back and moved me against him so I could feel his rock-hard erection pressing into my belly.

"I'd love to rip that dress off of you, but I don't think I can bear to. It's so beautiful." Lucas looked down at me, his eyes shining. "I don't know if I told you how stunning you are tonight. My heart literally stopped when I first saw you coming down the aisle."

"Thank you." My voice came out husky, and for some reason, I felt the pinpricks of tears.

He turned me around and gently unzipped the dress, letting it fall to the floor. Then he carefully hung it up before turning back to me. He grinned and motioned to the garter. "I forgot about that." He rubbed his thumb along it. "We might have to leave it on for now."

He kissed me again. Then I took off his jacket, unknotted his bow tie, unbuttoned his shirt, and undid his pants. I ran my hands down his gorgeous, chiseled chest reverently. I wanted to enjoy this moment. I wanted to memorize and save it for later, for when I was alone again.

I trailed my kisses lower, tracing his pectoral muscles with my tongue, and he moaned. I shivered with pure female satisfaction. He wanted *me.* He reached down and undid my bra—the lucky penny fell out and pinged against the floor, making me laugh throatily. "No pockets," I mumbled as his lips closed over mine again. He gently took my breasts in his hands, rubbing my nipples in circles with his thumbs. I leaned into him, moaning with ecstasy and relief. *This feels so right. I've been waiting for this.*

Lucas ran his hands over my body and pulled me against him. His erection, enormous and thick, pressed against my belly. His tongue searched my mouth, and I gave myself to him, surrendering to the urgency of his touch.

He laid me down on the bed, his glorious, naked body above me. Lucas pushed the hair off my face and just watched me for a moment, trailing a finger over my features as though he were memorizing them. Then he leaned in and kissed me again, deep and probing. I spread my legs a little, offering myself to him, yearning for him. He slid a finger inside of me slowly, testing me, and I moaned, bucking against him, wanting more. I grabbed his muscled ass and pulled him closer, running the head of his cock over my sex, getting it slick and wet, arching my back in an attempt to join our bodies.

"Please," I whispered.

"Like I could wait." Lucas entered me then, his hard

length filling me all at once, and I cried out. He buried himself in me, and my body stretched to accommodate his. He moved slowly at first, making sure I was comfortable with how big he was. I moaned, loving how he filled me. I ran my hands greedily down his muscled back. I'd been wanting to touch him more than I'd admitted to myself.

He thrust again, groaning, and my pussy quaked around him. I grabbed his ass and pushed him deeper into me, wanting to feel all of him, wanting him to overtake me. His body listened to mine. His long, deep strokes pushed me to the edge almost immediately.

He leaned up, and I drank in the sight of his taut, muscled body, the cords standing out on his neck. He didn't take his eyes off of me. I felt like he was trying to devour me with his body, and I was all for it. I was on the edge, my vision blurring around the edges as his thrusts got deeper and more urgent. I felt my orgasm circling me, large and powerful. "Come in me," I pleaded. "I want to feel you."

"Oh fuck. Blake." And then he did come, hard, filling me as my body clenched around him, and I cried out. He cursed as his body shuddered on top of me. After we stilled, Lucas rolled to the side and pulled me into his arms, cradling me against his chest.

His breathing became rhythmic and shallow as he

held me. As I started to drift off, I realized two things: I'd never orgasmed with a client before. Not ever. And I'd certainly never fallen asleep in one's arms.

LUCAS

I woke up with Blake in my arms. It was the strangest feeling. I was wearing a wedding band, and I had my arms wrapped around a beautiful woman, who happened to be my wife.

We'd consummated the marriage. Thank God I'd had a proper excuse, because now that we'd done it, I could finally admit to myself how much I'd wanted to. Since I'd met her, Blake had been all I could think about. When I'd seen her in her wedding dress last night, heading toward me, there was only one thing I'd wanted: her.

I watched her as she slept, her hair tumbling over the sheets. She looked beautiful and innocent. I looked at the engagement ring and wedding band on her hand, my mother's bangle still on her wrist. This seemed so real.

And if it seemed real to me, I probably didn't have to worry about Serena. Or anyone else.

I slid out of bed and grabbed my phone, shooting off a quick text to Jake:

Please tell everyone thanks for coming last night. My bride and I are staying in today, so we won't see you all off. Give everyone our love.

Jake responded immediately:

Did you give Blakey your love last night?

Much to my chagrin, he included a winking emoji.

With a frown, I tapped out a reply:

Fuck off. Go back to Washington.

I could practically see Jake leering as I read his next message:

Love you too, bro. Congratulations. You win. You have the hottest wife I've ever met.

I smiled a little at that. Then I ordered room service. When it arrived, I made sure everything was meticulously arranged before I headed back to the bedroom.

Blake was lying in bed, staring at her rings as if mesmerized. She jumped when I came in and stuck her hands back under the blankets. "Good morning." She sounded as if she were trying to play it cool.

"Good morning." I smiled at her. "Sorry to interrupt you."

"You didn't—oh well, yes you did. I was staring at how my rings sparkled." She sat up, smiling at me sheepishly, and I felt a rush just from looking at her.

"Are you hungry?"

She nodded. "I'm starving."

"Well, when you've finished admiring all available shiny objects, come out and join me in the dining room."

Blake sat up and looked at me skeptically. "You cooked?"

"Don't be crazy. I ordered room service, and I set it up on the table."

"Well, in that case," she said, smiling, "I'll be out in a minute."

She joined me exactly one minute later, wearing a T-shirt and a pair of leggings. Her hair was mussed. She sat down at the table and smiled at me shyly. "Hi."

"Hi." I tried to ignore the chills that shot through me when she smiled at me like that. "It's sort of awkward, right? We're newly married and newly consummated, all at once."

"It's totally sort of awkward. And awesome." Blake nodded, still smiling, and dug into her fruit cup. "Wouldn't it be nice to live at a hotel like this? You could always order whatever you want, whenever you want?"

"That's why I live at The Stratum. Room service twenty-four hours a day. And housekeeping."

Blake shook her head. "That's so not the real world. And neither is this." She looked around at the suite and the view beyond.

It's your world now, I thought. Blake deserved all the good things in life, and I was determined to give them to her this year. After that, the money I was paying her would help her have a bright, secure future.

One that didn't include me.

But I didn't want to think about that, so I pushed the thought roughly from my mind.

"If it's all right with you, I'd like us to stay in today. I think I've had enough company for one weekend."

Blake nodded. "Of course. When are we leaving for our trip?"

"Tomorrow morning." I couldn't wait to whisk her away to the beauty and peace of the islands. "So we have the day to ourselves to relax. I scheduled massages. Is there anything else you'd like to do?"

"I just want to check out that pool." She motioned to the deck outside. "It looks amazing."

"We can certainly do that." I pictured her in a bikini, and I felt a strong pull of desire in my belly. "Anything else? Do you like to gamble?"

"No," Blake said. "I don't like to take chances with money."

I smiled at her. "Me either. But how about we make plans to go to dinner? Just the two of us?" The hopeful tone in my voice disgusted me. *Who else is she going to hang out with?*

She smiled at me. "That sounds great. Everything

was wonderful yesterday, but I'm definitely feeling wiped out from it all."

"Me too."

We finished breakfast in silence. I couldn't tell if it was awkward or not. "You want to hit the pool?" I asked.

Blake flashed another smile at me, putting me at ease. "That sounds great." She headed off to change, and I mentally kicked myself. I was acting like a crushed-out schoolboy, for Christ's sake. We met outside on the private deck, which overlooked the strip. The sun was climbing in the sky, but the temperature was still perfect, warm without being overbearing.

"This is so amazing," Blake said. "I never even knew that a hotel room could have its own pool." She stripped off her cover-up to reveal a black string bikini, and any response I might have been formulating froze on my lips. She noticed me watching her and tossed her hair over her shoulder. "What?" she asked nonchalantly as she stepped into the pool. Her nipples immediately hardened underneath the scraps of fabric covering them.

I felt myself getting hard again. "Is it cold?"

Blake went all the way into the water, splashing a little. "No, it's amazing. You should come in."

She didn't need to ask me twice. I stripped out of my T-shirt and headed into the water, hoping it was cold enough to calm man-land. Blake went under and then sat on one side of the pool. I climbed in and sat on the other.

"So… this is still awkward, right?" she asked.

"Seems to be." Another silence ensued. This one was definitely awkward.

Blake watched me from her side. "So, here's the state of our union, as I see it. We got married, and we had sex last night. And you said that we only had to consummate once in order for the marriage to be legal. So where does that leave us?"

"In a pool designed for sin. In Vegas. And you in that sexy bikini," I said, deadpan.

She tossed her hair again. "I don't own any other kind. It's not like I'm trying to tempt you, I swear."

I groaned and leaned back against the edge of the pool. She didn't have to try. My cock was already rock-hard, pointing straight in her direction as if in salute. "So, what are you asking me?"

"I'm just trying to understand the parameters," she said simply. "I like to know where I stand."

"Then come here. I'll show you where to stand," I growled.

Blake arched an eyebrow but complied, moving slowly across the pool until she was standing closer. "Yes… sir?"

My dick was throbbing as I watched her tits bob in the water, so tantalizingly close. "What if I change the rules?"

I watched her throat work as she swallowed. "To what?"

I stood up and closed the distance between us, fingering the delicate strap of her bikini. "What if I asked you to share my bed for the next week? While we're on our honeymoon?"

Blake looked up at me expectantly, her lips slightly parted, her cheeks flushing. "And then?"

"And then we'll revisit the situation," I said smoothly. The assurance in my voice was false. I had no idea what I was doing. What I *did* know was that I needed to be inside her again. Right now. And that maybe, if I let myself have her for this next week, I could get my fill of her body.

"That sounds reasonable." Her voice was even, but her pupils were dilated, and her nipples were hard. She wanted me, too. And it wasn't an act for my benefit. It wasn't an ego boost for a client. I could see her trembling slightly, and it filled me with satisfaction.

I was going to make her scream my name, all day, every day, for a whole week. Once I was done with her, she was never going to forget about me.

This was for better or for worse, after all.

I reached for her, running my thumb along her bottom lip. She bit it softly and then came to me, pressing herself against my body.

I leaned down and kissed her, my hands roving hungrily over her skin. I didn't know if I would be able to get enough of this. Of her. There was an urgency in her kiss, too. She rubbed her breasts against me, arching her back and moaning. I couldn't wait. I reached down, stripped off her bikini bottom, and lifted her up. She instinctively wrapped her legs around me, and I moved us back to the edge of the pool. I lifted her out of the water and sat her on the edge, delicately spreading her legs apart. Then I sunk lower in the water until her naked sex was level with my face. I ran my tongue along her perfect pink slit, and she cried out, throwing her head back. Her taste was mesmerizing, sweet and musky. I buried my face in her, licking and tonguing her clitoris.

"Lucas!" she said, breathless, as I took her clit in between my teeth, biting her a little.

Then I slid two fingers inside her. Her pussy quaked around them. "Oh, *fuck*," she moaned. I drew my fingers out and plunged them back in. She was slick with wetness, and not just from the pool.

Her body moved to meet my hand. I smiled into her

pussy and teased her with my tongue some more. "You like that?"

"I like your cock better," she panted. Still, she came, hard, the next time I stroked her insides with my fingers and planted my mouth on her clit.

"You can have it now, babe." I pulled my swim trunks off and positioned one leg up on the side of the pool. Then I slid my throbbing dick toward her entrance.

She watched me, her eyes huge in her face. "Lucas… I need you." Her voice was thick. She arched her back, spread her pussy open, and started fingering her clit. For some reason, that almost undid me. I eased myself into her, feeling her body stretch for me. I thrust slowly at first, but soon Blake was grabbing my ass, pulling me in deeper, begging me to give it to her harder. She was driving me absofuckinglutely wild. The horizon tipped as she moaned and rode my cock, calling my name, her pussy spasming around me.

"Blake… oh fuck, Blake, what're you doing to me?" I heard myself ask lowly as my orgasm built all around me. Our bodies slammed together, hard, until I pulled back and we did it again. And again. I was in deep, so deep, and my thrusts were becoming longer now. I was almost there. I fingered Blake's clit hard, almost cruelly, and her body erupted in spasms against mine.

And then I came in her, hot and hard.

Later, in bed, after we'd made love again, Blake nudged me gently. "What," I said, too spent to make it sound like a question.

"I forgot to tell you something," she said.

"What's that?" I was on the edge of sleep, but I pulled her warm body closer, so I could feel her.

"I like you, Lucas. I forgot to tell you that I like you, too."

BLAKE

The next twenty-four hours passed in a blur of luxury and constant contact. We'd had dinner at an amazing Japanese restaurant, we'd had sex on every available surface in the suite, and I'd had more orgasms than I could count. And we hadn't stopped touching each other. We'd even showered together, making love with the hot water pouring over us.

And I'd told Lucas that I liked him, idiot that I was. It was the truth, but in this case, the truth hadn't set me free. It was like a vise-grip around my heart. I was suddenly aware that our fake relationship seemed awfully real and important to me.

Still, I didn't seem to be alone in wanting to always be touching. Lucas held my hand on our entire private flight to our honeymoon destination. I'd caught him looking at me several times, tracing the planes of my face with his eyes, as if he were memorizing me.

I had no idea where the plane was headed. "Where are we going?" I asked. "Maine?"

"I'll take you to Maine later this summer," he said. "We're going to an island first."

"Oh." I attempted to sound casual, as if island-hopping was something I did all the time.

"You'll like it. I promise. There's food. And pools." He smirked at me but then reached over and pulled me against him, kissing the top of my head. He'd said he didn't like to be close to other people, but ever since we'd opened the floodgates, he'd been nothing but affectionate. I hated to admit it, but I loved it; I felt as though I was blooming underneath his attention. I laid my head against his chest, loving the feel of his muscles, his warmth. It felt so good to relax and be held by someone I genuinely liked. It was the first time I'd ever experienced anything like it.

I peered out the window at the turquoise water below. "Okay, we're definitely going to the Caribbean."

He smiled at me indulgently, making my heart flip. "For a blonde, you're actually pretty smart," he teased.

"Ha ha," I said. "Did you ever hear this one? What's black, blue, and brown, and lying in a ditch?"

"No."

"A brunette who's told too many blonde jokes," I said. "You'd do well to remember that."

Lucas smiled at me, his dimple flashing. "I like it when you're feisty."

"That's probably good. You seem to bring it out in me. Now, will you *please* tell me where we're going?"

"No." He playfully pulled me onto his lap. "Do you need me to say that more slowly because you're a natural blonde?"

"This could be a very long trip," I deadpanned.

Eventually, the flight attendant came out. She raised her eyebrow when she saw me nestled on Lucas's lap. "We'll be landing soon. Please fasten your seat belts."

I felt my face flush as I scrambled back into my seat and secured my seat belt. Properly chastised, I went back to looking out the window. I traced the outline of the island below with my fingertip. "Turks and Caicos," I finally said, triumphant.

"How did you know?" Lucas asked.

I pointed out the window. "Because I can see it."

"Have you been here before?"

"Never," I turned back to the window and stared out at the turquoise water. "But I've always wanted to."

"Then this is even more perfect." Lucas linked his fingers through mine. "It's one of my favorite places."

A driver was waiting for us at the airport. "Mr. Ford, it's a pleasure to see you again."

"Davian. Nice to see you."

I shot him a look. "You have a regular driver on an exotic island?"

"I own a home here," he said without looking at me.

"You *what*? When were you going to surprise me with this one?"

"Today," Lucas said. "So are you? Surprised?"

"I'm basically suspending disbelief at this point." I smiled at him and accepted Davian's hand as he lifted me up to the SUV.

Lucas slid in behind me, his dimple flashing intermittently as I oohed and aahed over the island—the trees, the colorful houses, the amazing white sand beaches. "It's paradise," I said.

Lucas ran his fingers down my back, making me shiver and making me feel hot at the same time. I was never going to forget this.

I didn't ever want to forget this.

After a twenty-minute drive, Davian pulled up to an intricate wrought-iron gate and punched in a code. "The staff will be happy to see you. Everyone's excited, Mr. and Mrs. Ford. Congratulations." He smiled at us in the rearview mirror, his teeth flashing.

"Thank you, Davian." We drove down a long drive,

shaded by palms, and pulled up in front of a massive estate.

"This is your *home*?" I asked. "Your second—no wait, your *third* home?" It was enormous, stone-faced, and stately. He needed to pay me more.

He shrugged. "I bought it for tax purposes."

"That's some tax bill." How much money did Lucas already *have*? And he'd married me so he could inherit even more? I was *so* asking for a raise.

We parked, and Davian held out his hand for me. But Lucas stepped in, pulling me protectively against him.

"You don't have to protect me from your driver," I teased lowly. "I promise I won't like holding anybody's hand better than yours."

He still kept me close. "I just like having you next to me. Is that okay?"

My insides warmed. "Of course it's okay."

We ascended the massive stone steps and entered the house, which was formal and imposing on the outside but warm and cheerful on the inside—thanks in large part to the smiling staff that was assembled within. "Mr. Ford!" they called. One of the women wrapped her arms around me and gave me a huge hug. "Mrs. Ford. Welcome. And congratulations."

Lucas was reserved in his gratitude toward everyone,

but I saw his dimple creeping out. He was genuinely pleased.

"Come on, now," Davian said to us after we'd been hugged and congratulated and generally fussed over. "I know Mr. Ford likes his privacy. We'll leave you two in peace, I promise. We've been here all weekend. The house has been cleaned and fully stocked. Your dinner has been prepared. You'll have the entire property to yourself in no time. Housekeeping will come back tomorrow, and you know I'm always just a text away."

Davian threw open the double doors that led to the tremendous interior courtyard and infinity pool. I marveled at the gorgeous view of the white sand beach beyond. Davian smiled at the delighted expression on my face. "Enjoy your stay, Mrs. Ford. I'll see you soon."

And with that, he was gone. Then it was just Lucas and me, his infinity pool, and the amazing view of the water.

"This is the most beautiful place I've ever seen." I felt overwhelmed.

"Do you want to swim?" Lucas sounded excited. He was already stripping out of his clothes.

"I'm going to *live* in this water," I said. "Are you kidding me?" The ocean back East was freezing, even in August. I'd never even seen a pool like this before, not to mention the aqua waters beyond, except in magazines and movies.

"Go grab your suit." He pulled me in for a quick, hot kiss that left me wanting more. "I'll be waiting."

I practically ran to get changed. By the time I got back, he was already in the pool, and a bottle of champagne was chilling on a table nearby. "Slowpoke," he called. I could see the chiseled lines of his chest glinting in the sun.

"I had to check out the house," I said, wading into the water. "It's amazing, Lucas. I wish we were going to live here for the whole year."

"I'm glad you like it. We can come back whenever I can get away from work." He grinned at me as I got closer, then I couldn't wait anymore—I dove underwater to close the distance between us. I sprung up when I reached him, and he yelped. And then I threw my arms around his neck and kissed him, unrestrained. The strange and overwhelming feeling of unbridled happiness filled my heart.

My heart was so full just from being next to him.

He pulled me into his arms, and we waded through the pool. Then he picked me up and carried me to the beach, where I swam in the warm, turquoise waters of the Caribbean for the first time in my life.

LUCAS

We had sex in the pool, sex in the hot tub, sex on the beach... sex in my bed. But the best part was having dinner outside, under the stars, with no city noise, no lights, and no distractions. Just me and Blake, with delicious jerk-flavored grouper and a grilled papaya salad. And then we tumbled into bed together, our limbs entangled. The addictive, brain-addling smell of her hair washed over me, and her soft, warm body pressed against mine.

Fuck. I was falling for her. I fucking knew it.

"Lucas?" she asked, breaking my reverie.

"What, baby?" I stroked her back. I couldn't help myself. I had to touch her. I had to have her next to me all the time.

"Do you bring lots of women here?" she asked in a husky voice.

"No." The question bothered me. I'd never brought anyone else here in the two years I'd owned the place. I felt exposed. "I usually just come down alone, to unwind."

"Were you lonely?" she asked, stroking my chest.

"No." I was quiet for a moment. "Yes. I don't know."

"I've been alone my whole life." She rolled away from

me and pulled my arm over her shoulder so I was still holding her close. "But I never thought I was lonely." She nestled against me, yawning. "Now I know that I was."

She fell asleep then, but I stayed up for a long time, just thinking about her words.

I didn't want to let go of her, and I didn't want her to be lonely. And those were two things I couldn't afford to want—maybe the only two things in the world I couldn't afford.

"WOULD YOU LIKE TO GO SNORKELING?" I asked Blake after breakfast the next morning.

"I don't know. I've never been," she said.

"You can do it," I assured her. "We'll take the boat out, and I can show you."

"Is it your boat—oh never mind," she said. "Of course it's your boat."

"It's totally my boat." I held out my hand for her. "Come."

She looked at me coyly and took my hand. "Yes, sir."

"You're going to pay for that. Later."

She tossed her hair. "Don't mind if I do."

I had a private dock for my boat. I texted the captain I sometimes hired to meet us there. We grabbed the picnic lunch that housekeeping had prepared for us, as well as several bottles of wine and sunscreen, and headed over to the boat.

It was a perfect day. The sun shone brightly, there was a slight breeze, and I was holding Blake's hand.

Jesus. I couldn't believe the turn my thoughts were taking. I was turning into such a girl I should have packed a bra and a box of tampons for this trip.

My crew of two were waiting for us at the boat. "Where do you want to go today, Mr. Ford?" the captain asked.

"I was thinking French Cay. My wife's never been snorkeling before." My gut twisted with pride at the word *wife*.

"You'll love it," both men said, nodding solemnly at Blake. "French Cay is the most beautiful spot. No construction. We might even see dolphins on the way."

"Really?" Blake clapped her hands, looking as excited as a small child.

The captain grinned at her. "Really. Now you two relax and enjoy your honeymoon. We'll take care of you."

Even though I'd been out on the water many times, seeing Blake's awed expression made the scenery come alive to me again. She stayed pressed against me, her hand clutching mine, as she watched the lush island disappear from view and the translucent, turquoise water surround us. "So beautiful," she said.

"I know." But I was only looking at her.

"There they are," the captain called, pointing behind us. "A whole pod."

There was a group of dolphins behind us, jumping out of the water every so often.

"Oh my God!" Blake said, watching them with delight.

"They're showing off for you," I said.

She pulled up her sunglasses, and I could see that her eyes were sparkling. "I can't believe it. They're so cool."

I couldn't help but smile. Her unabashed enthusiasm was infectious.

The dolphins followed us for a while, and we parted ways when we reached French Cay. It was a small, low-lying uninhabited island. The captain motored the boat expertly toward an inlet. We were out in open water, but we would be safe snorkeling close to the boat.

"Are you ready?" I asked Blake. I'd helped her assemble her mask and snorkel, and the captain had talked her through the basics.

Two hectic spots of color dotted her cheeks. "I think so."

"You'll be fine, babe. It's fun."

She nodded at me. "I'm excited." But she looked

nervous as she followed me down the ladder to the water. I waited for her, treading water patiently. The wind had picked up a little bit, and the typically calm water had a bit of a roll to it, but it wasn't too bad. Blake seemed reluctant to let go of the ladder, but she finally did, paddling out to me cautiously.

"You okay?" I asked.

She nodded and adjusted her mask.

"Just follow me." I fit the snorkel into my mouth and swam over to her, making sure hers fit comfortably. She just nodded and gave me the thumbs up. "Let's do it." I put my face in the water and swam calmly toward the reef with Blake beside me.

Colorful fish swam past in groups. More were feasting on the bright, almost fluorescent coral. I pointed out a parrot fish, an angel fish, and a turtle. Blake nodded each time, keeping pace. We swam farther out, and I took out my mouthpiece in order to dive down.

I was examining some sort of triangular-looking fish when I heard what sounded like Blake screaming. I turned around in a panic.

She'd come underwater, but she was struggling to get back to the top. Her mouth was open, and I could hear her shrieking, even though it was muffled. I headed toward her then saw what she was upset about. A large barracuda, silver and sparkling in the sunlight, swam very close to her. Its spiky, needle-sharp teeth poked out of its mouth menacingly. It wouldn't likely go after her, but I could see why she was afraid of it.

I broke the surface of the water, and she was next to me, arms flailing. "Blake."

She went under then popped back up a moment later, barely catching her breath before disappearing again.

"Blake!" I swam to her swiftly, my arms cutting through the water, and grabbed her just before she went under again. I held her up and swam back to the boat. The captain and his first mate were shouting at me. The captain jumped in the water and helped me pull Blake up the ladder. She was spluttering and crying.

I managed to get the mask off her then checked her vitals. "I'm fine," she said, crying. "That fish just scared me, and then I panicked."

Once I was sure she wasn't in any physical danger, I wrapped her in a towel and brought her to the back of the boat, cradling her in my arms. She clung to me, still crying. "I'm sorry." She wiped her eyes.

I felt as if my heart was being squeezed. "Are you hurt?"

Her eyes were red, spilling over with fresh tears. "No, I'm just embarrassed."

I wiped the tears from her cheeks. "You've got nothing to be embarrassed about. I forgot to warn you that we might see a barracuda. And diving in open water like this on a windy day—that was a stupid idea. A selfish one. I'm so sorry." I pulled her closer, and she clung to me.

She let out a bark of laughter. "Five-year-olds snorkel, babe. I'm the one who should be sorry." She buried herself in my chest. "Just don't let that thing near me ever again! Did you see its *teeth*? Did you see its *eyes*? They were flat and shiny, like deadly nickels—"

"Shhh." I rocked her back and forth. "I saw it. I'm going to come back later and put a spear through it."

"Not without me." She shuddered. "I'm going to be the one to do it."

"No." I stroked her hair. "I'm keeping you safe from now on." *Till death do us part.* It hadn't even been a week, and I was falling. Hard. She leaned up and kissed my cheek, and I wrapped my arms even tighter around her, still cursing myself for ever putting her at risk.

BLAKE

That barracuda had scared the bejeebles out of me.

But what was even worse? The way I'd clung to Lucas as if he was the last life preserver on Earth. I never depended on anyone but myself. I'd learned the hard way that was the only way to make it through this world. But I'd been playing a dangerous game these last few days, and it was starting to catch up to me.

Once we'd gotten home, Lucas had put me in the shower and washed my hair. He was tender with his attention, taking care of me. He must've asked me ten times if I was really okay. I was okay with the barracuda —and I was totally serious about putting a spear in the thing myself—but I was not okay with what was going on inside of me.

I didn't want to be away from Lucas. I wanted to have breakfast, lunch, and dinner with him. I wanted to sit on his lap. I wanted him inside me all the time. I had an undeniable craving for his body. We'd been having sex until I was sore, but still, it wasn't enough.

After we showered and Lucas watched me dry my hair, claiming he didn't want to leave me alone, he led me to bed. "Let's just watch a movie and chill for a little while," he said. "I think we've had enough excitement for one day."

"Okay," I said agreeably. But the fire raging between my legs told a different story—I was, in fact, ready for more excitement. I dropped the towel on the floor and climbed, naked, onto the bed.

"What are you doing?" he asked, watching me with hooded eyes.

"Relaxing." I crawled up toward where he was propped up on the bed and straddled him. I could feel him, already hard and thick beneath me.

"You need to rest." He attempted to gently lift me from his lap, but I clamped my thighs against him stubbornly.

"Don't make such a big deal out of it. I'm fine."

He took a lock of my hair in between his fingers and stroked it. "I was worried about you," he said in a soft voice. "When I saw you go back underwater... it was scary."

I leaned forward and kissed his nose. "Then maybe *you're* the one who needs to relax."

He smiled at me, his dimple showing. "I think I'm recovered enough."

I arched an eyebrow at him. "Enough for what?"

He put his hands on my ass and pulled me forward so that his erection rubbed me through his mesh shorts. "I think you know, Blakey."

"If you weren't so handsome and well-endowed, you'd seriously be bugging me with that nickname by now."

"Lucky for me," Lucas said in a teasing tone.

"And me." I grinned at him then leaned in for a lingering kiss. Our tongues connected gently at first and then with more urgency.

I pulled his shorts off and arranged our naked bodies against each other. We both practically sighed in relief. This felt right. As I slid his cock into me and started to ride him, pleasure ripped through me. And I realized one thing: this felt too good to be true.

But I was going to let myself have it, even if it was just for right now.

LUCAS

We went back to French Cay the next day.

"You sure you want to go back in there?" Billy asked Blake, his eyes searching hers. "I can take you over to Smith's Reef. We can snorkel right from the beach."

"I need to get over my fear," she said bravely. "We're in paradise, right? What good is it if I'm too afraid to explore the world around me? I live in Boston, for Christ's sake. It's freezing there ninety percent of the time."

With that, Blake pulled her mask down, stepped up on the edge of the boat in her flippers, and jumped into the water.

"Do you want me to come in?" the captain asked me, watching for Blake below.

"I got her." *I think.* I jumped in the water after her, and my heart rate was already skyrocketing. Blake was determined, that was for damn sure. I adjusted my snorkel and went underwater. She was right below the surface, looking at a rainbow fish. When she saw me, she smiled, and it felt like the sun coming out. Heavenly.

She reached out for my hand, and I took it. Then we swam together, like newlyweds, to explore the reef.

There wasn't a barracuda in sight. The captain said he knew the one we'd seen the day before—his nick-name was Dwayne and he was often spotted near this reef. I looked around the water for him, but he never came out.

Someday, Dwayne, I thought.

BLAKE

"The trip was wonderful, Elena. It was amazing." I ran my hands through my hair and looked out the window at the Boston Common, wishing we were still on the island and that I had Lucas all to myself. "Nikki and the rest of the girls did a great job at the wedding. The whole thing was perfect."

"Nikki said they behaved," Elena said. "Did they?"

"Absolutely," I lied.

"This is the most money we've ever made from one client," she said. "If you can keep him happy, he could be a huge source for referrals going forward."

"He seems happy. I think so, anyway. We haven't had any trouble with his family since the wedding." I was glad Elena couldn't see my furrowed brow. We hadn't heard a word from Serena, which unsettled me. She'd been polite to me at the wedding, almost friendly. But I knew she would never sit by and watch Lucas inherit half of all that money without some sort of fight.

"Good. Let's stay in touch. Check in with me if you need anything. Otherwise, I'll call you in a few weeks."

We hung up, and I called my mother next. I looked at my rings, feeling guilty. I couldn't even send her a picture without breaching my confidentiality clause. She would never see me in that wedding dress or see the happy smile that had graced my lips.

Maybe it was better that way.

She answered on the first ring. "Honey, hi! I'm so glad you called. I missed you so much." She paused to cough for a moment, a deep, congested sound.

"Are you okay?"

She waited until her coughing subsided to speak. "I've just been a little off-kilter this week, but I'm fine. I'm taking my medicine. I'm doing all the right things... It's just the humidity, I think."

New England summers were notoriously humid, but that wasn't why she sounded so congested. "You need to call the doctor."

"I don't need to do any such thing. Your sister's here, taking care of me." Her cheerfulness sounded forced.

"What the fuck is Chelsea still doing there?" I hissed, the words tumbling out before I could stop them. My mother hated it when I cursed, and she hated it even worse when I cursed about my sister.

"Blake—*stop* it."

"What's her highness saying about me now?" I heard Chelsea ask sharply from the background. I could just picture them sitting in my dingy kitchen, the cheerful drapes from Target failing to mask the moldy window frames and the view of the paint-peeling, multi-family housing unit smack dab next door.

"We saw your picture in the paper," my mother said tightly. "You look beautiful."

My heart sank at the word *we.* I glimpsed at the *Globe,* lying open to our wedding announcement, which displayed a gorgeous picture of Lucas and me from our photo shoot in the park. The article listed all of Lucas's accolades and was packed with lies about me. "Oh. Thanks."

"Let me talk to her," my sister snapped, grabbing the phone. "You're *married*? To a *billionaire*?"

"Um… yep." I had no idea what my mother had told her.

"Since *when*?" I could almost see the look of complete indignity warping my sister's pretty face.

"Since Lucas asked me to marry him and we got married last week."

"Why didn't you invite Mom?"

"I couldn't," I said quickly. *What had my mother told her?* "Lucas and I wanted… to keep it private."

Chelsea snorted. "You had a hundred people at the

'small, intimate and luxurious' Vegas ceremony," she quoted. "Did you feel like you needed to keep the riffraff out?"

"That's why *you* didn't get invited," I said, unable to hold back. Chelsea always knew how to push my buttons. "Mom couldn't come because she was too sick to travel."

"Everything in the announcement about you is a lie," she said. "You're a *hooker,* not a branding expert with a degree from UNH. The only advanced degree you have is in deep throating."

"*Chelsea*!" My mother sounded horrified.

"Well, it's true. She's a freaking hooker, Mom! Don't act like you don't know it." I practically heard my sister toss her hair. "Maybe you should fill me in on exactly what's going on."

"I'd love to, but I have to go now."

"We should do lunch, you know? Now that you're big time. Take your sister out for a meal on Newbury Street. When was the last time you did something nice for me?"

"I bought you a wedding present when you got married to Vince," I reminded her. "I thought that was pretty giving of me."

"You're really never going to let that go? Vince is a *douche,* and you know it."

But he'd been my douche. Vince had been my first everything—first love, first time. I was only seventeen when I'd met him. I didn't realize what a complete jack-hole he was until my sister stole him out from under me right before our wedding and married him herself.

I would have appreciated the opportunity to figure out the extent of his douchiness for myself.

"I've let it go." *Sheesh, I'm lying a lot for one day.* "But I don't really see where you get this entitlement from. What have you done for *me* lately?"

"I haven't called the *Globe* and told them the truth about you." Her words came out too quickly, as though she'd already been contemplating doing just that. "And I haven't called that handsome husband of yours, either, to tell him all about where you really come from."

"You stay away from him."

"What're you worried about, huh? That he might wanna taste of the hotter sister, too?"

Chelsea, your complete lack of remorse shows what a total DOUCHEPANTS-O-RAMA you are.

But I didn't say that. I didn't want to start World War III. "No," I said in as controlled a fashion as I could manage. "I'm pretty sure Lucas thinks *I'm* the hotter sister."

"Well then, you don't need to hide me from him."

Jesus, she didn't take no for an answer. "We're really busy right now. But I'll call you when I can get together. Why is Mom so congested?" I asked, desperate to change the subject.

"Who knows," Chelsea said and yawned. "It's not like it's anything new. She'll be fine."

"You're really something special, you know that?"

"Oh yeah. I know that. I'll be in touch." She hung up before I could tell her not to bother, not ever.

This was just what I needed. Lucas was the best thing to ever happen to me, and now my dead-beat sister had caught a whiff of opportunity. She was probably going to try to leech onto me and suck out whatever she could —a lunch on Newbury street, the opportunity to flirt with my rich, handsome husband.

She also couldn't pass up the chance to threaten outing me as an escort in order to see what she could squeeze out of me in return. Money. Clothes. Attention. The list of things my sister wanted was endless, as was her list of excuses for why she couldn't hold down a job and obtain them for herself.

I put my face into my hands as the high I'd been feeling since the wedding came crashing down around me. Just when I thought I'd put some distance between myself and my past, it seemed poised to attack me like a zombie, ready to eat me and everyone else near me alive.

I decided to hit the gym while I waited for Lucas to get home from work. At least if I kept in good shape, I had a chance of running away from my problems for just a little longer.

LUCAS

"Mr. Ford, there's a Rupert Granger for you on line one," the receptionist said.

"Put him through." In the brief moment before he clicked over, I looked out my office window and saw that late-afternoon thunderclouds had gathered over the city.

"Lucas. How's married life treating you?"

"It's great, Rupert. Thanks for making the trip out to the wedding. It meant a lot."

"You probably know this isn't a social call."

I nodded to myself. No one called me to chat, not even my wife.

"Serena's attorney sent me a letter today. They're preparing an investigation into the validity of the trust provisions. As the trust administrator, I have a duty to disclose that to you."

He caught me off guard. "What's the basis for that?"

"They're not contesting the validity of your marriage," Rupert explained. "They're contesting the validity of the trust provisions themselves. Her attorney said he found a recent case that might make the provisions void in the state of Massachusetts."

For some reason, my stomach sank. "But this is just a preliminary investigation."

"Yes, but this could have ramifications for both of you. Soon. The attorney said they were going to look into other jurisdictions and see if there are any similar precedents. I'm just calling you as a courtesy, but also to let you know that if these provisions are deemed void or voidable, you and Serena will immediately inherit the trust. I won't use trust funds to put up a legal fight—your mother wouldn't have wanted that, and as her executor, it's my duty to carry out her wishes."

"Let me get this straight... if the courts are ruling that provisions like these are no longer enforceable, ours are considered void?" I asked.

"Right. And if the social provisions of the trust are deemed void, and there won't be any threshold to meet," Rupert explained. "In other words, Serena's previous marriage doesn't affect her ability to inherit the money, and it won't matter if you and Blake stay married for a year, although I certainly hope you do."

I scrubbed my hand across my face. This didn't make sense. Serena was already free and clear to inherit. "Why would Serena want to do this, especially since she's already complied with the terms?"

Rupert cleared his throat. "I'm not at liberty to discuss that. You'll have to ask her directly."

"Okay…" I paused for a beat, my mind racing. Serena wouldn't be forthcoming with me about her reasons, and I knew it. "You know my mother didn't like family secrets. The least you could do is give me some sort of idea… to honor her memory."

"I have a fiduciary duty to protect the grantee's best interests—and in this instance, I mean your sister's." Rupert sounded annoyed. "So the only thing I'll tell you is that something happened with Robert. I don't know anything more than that. I'll keep you up to date about the inquiry. Good day, Lucas."

I mumbled a good-bye and stalked to the window. It had started to pour, and steam was rising from the late-summer pavement. *What in the world is going on with my sister?*

In a very un-Lucas-like move, I picked up my phone and called her.

In a typical Serena move, she let it go straight to voice mail.

Frustrated, I decided to head for home. I could take Blake to dinner, ravage her sexy body, and maybe then I would be able to think straight. Of course, that was just an excuse. Since we'd been back from the island, I hadn't stayed at the office past five. I couldn't stand to be away from her.

Stop and buy yourself a box of tampons and a bag of chocolates on your way home, I remonstrated myself.

But the new me didn't care. I was married to a gorgeous woman, I was getting laid every night, and for once, I wasn't in a bad fucking mood.

I TOLD Blake about the call from Rupert over dinner. "Why don't you call Robert?" she suggested.

"That might be an option," I said. "Although I doubt she's told him anything."

"They were having some deep discussion at the wedding." Blake poured us each a glass of wine. "You can at least find out what that was about. Or do you want me to reach out to Serena? She was actually pretty decent toward me after she'd had two bottles of wine."

"I wouldn't do that to you. I'll handle it."

Later, after Blake was asleep, I padded out to the kitchen. Rupert's phone call was seriously troubling me, and I couldn't put my finger on why. I looked at the clock. Robert was a night owl; he would definitely still be up at this hour.

He picked up after the first ring. "Lucas, to what do I owe this honor?"

I poured myself a drink and sat down. "I'm just checking in with you."

He snorted. "Since when?"

"Since I saw you huddled in a corner with my sister at my wedding. And now she's not returning my calls."

"Since when did she ever return your calls?"

"Never. But the silence is particularly deafening right now." I enjoyed the burn of my drink going down. "The trust administrator called me today. He said that Serena's attorney had been in touch."

Robert didn't say anything for a moment. "Did he say why?"

"He said that the attorney was investigating a new case that could make the trust's terms voidable."

"I see," Robert said.

"What do you see, exactly?"

He sighed. "What do you want from me? I'm not married to her anymore. I thought that one of the benefits of my divorce was that I was excused from your crazy family's drama."

"I still consider you a friend, Robert. And the administrator mentioned your name."

"We are friends. As a result, I'm comfortable telling you that I have nothing to say on the matter. I have to go."

"Talk soon?"

"Do we have to?"

"Until I get the answers I'm looking for, I'm keeping your number at the top of my contact list."

"Great." His voice was grim.

"Love the enthusiasm. I get that a lot."

"I'll bet." He hung up before I could bother him further. I drained my glass and headed back to bed. My sister was going to get a surprise, and most unwelcome, visit from her little brother tomorrow.

MY DRIVER INTERCEPTED Serena when she left her office to get sushi. Her "office" was really just her townhouse, from which she shopped online and organized cocktail parties. He motioned toward the car, and she stuck her head in, scowling. "Ugh, what do *you* want?"

I patted the seat beside me. "I just want to take you to lunch."

She groaned but slid in. "So it begins. Your full-of-shit fest."

"Come on now," I said. "You're about to hurt my feelings."

"We both know you have no feelings."

"You wound me." I gave her a fake pout.

"Jesus." She rolled her eyes. "Being married's made you even more of an asshole."

"Enough," I said, already tired of pretending to be nice. "I picked you up for a reason."

Serena gave me a satisfied smile. "Of course you did."

"I spoke to Robert last night."

Her eyes almost popped out of her head. A master of disguise, she recovered quickly, composing her face and picking an invisible speck of lint off her black jumpsuit. "Oh, really? How is good old Robert?"

"Why don't you tell me, Serena?"

She gave me an ugly look. "Are you really buying me lunch?"

"Only if I have to."

"You have to. I was headed to O Ya."

O Ya was the most exclusive Japanese restaurant in the city. "Are they open for lunch?"

She shrugged with fake nonchalance. "For certain

customers."

We drove through the Leather District, and Ian let us out in front of the restaurant. The stunning hostess kissed my sister on both cheeks and immediately seated us in a sleek booth. For a restaurant that stated on its website that it was only open for dinner, O Ya had a pretty full lunch crowd of Boston's beautiful people.

Serena ordered the chef's tasting of sashimi and a $1,500 bottle of Veuve Clicquot champagne. "Glad you're buying." She motioned for the waiter to fill her glass.

"I'm only buying if this is actually beneficial. And I don't consider watching you day-drink in a jumpsuit particularly productive."

"Well then… let's get productive, shall we?" She took a healthy swallow and put her glass down then leaned toward me across the table. "I'll cut right to the chase. I found out about you. About Blake."

I grabbed the champagne and filled my glass to the brim. "Found out what?"

"About her… *you know*… questionable work history." Her voice was a whisper, and her cheeks were flushed.

Fuck. I wanted to reach across the table and throttle her, but something was off. Her tone was almost gentle. She wasn't flashing me an evil grin and going in for the kill.

That was not like my sister, not at all.

I decided to play straight with her. "What about it?"

Her throat worked as she swallowed more champagne. "I had her investigated before the wedding, right after that first dinner. I knew there was no way a woman *that* gorgeous had flown below my radar until you somehow plucked her from obscurity. Something was definitely off. So I looked into it."

I had to protect Blake. When my sister got a hold of something, she was like an Armani-collared dog with a bone. "What do you want, Serena?"

"You can't give me what I want, because I already screwed this up." She shook her head, her cheeks heating and her eyes glistening. "I should've come to you first. Instead, I got so drunk at your wedding that I blathered on and on about my plan to ruin you to Robert." She sat back and swiped at her face.

I was baffled. *Is my sister crying?* "And?"

Serena carefully wiped her face again, keeping her makeup intact, and drained her glass. "*And* he said that you looked happy."

"So?"

Serena sniffled. "He said he'd never seen you look happy before."

I wasn't sure where this was going. "So..."

"He said he'd out me if I went after you. For

marrying him and staying married to him because I had to." Serena didn't wait for the waiter to come back; she just filled her glass and kept the bottle within reach. "Because our marriage wasn't real. It wasn't real, and I divorced him as soon as I felt like I could."

Well, well, well. I crossed my arms against my chest and calmly regarded my sister. "So you cheated the trust provisions."

"I cheated. Just like you did." She sniffled again. I couldn't ascertain why she was upset—if it was about the money or something else, like the fact that Robert had thwarted her plans.

"I thought your marriage to Robert was real."

"It got a little too real, to be honest. He wanted me to stay home, be boring and get pregnant. But I'm sorry, I just couldn't tolerate that! He was asking me to be normal, and I'm not made for that." She pushed her sashimi around on her plate without taking a bite. "On top of that, I was starting to like him more than I should. It was getting sort of gross."

I decided to keep my mouth shut about the fact that she'd been married to him, and that liking him was hardly a problem. This was Serena after all, who lived in the land of $1,500 bottles of champagne at lunch and no common sense. "But how could he *out* you? Where's the proof? You dated him; you married him."

She raised her eyes to look into mine. "*I* asked *him* to marry *me* in exchange for five million dollars."

I sat back. "And he said *yes?*" Robert was wealthy in his own right; he was a doctor because he loved it, but he had his own family money. And I'd never seen him act as though he loved money or the spotlight. He'd acted as if he loved Serena, though. Had he fooled me for all these years?

She shook her head. "He said no. But then he proposed because he said he loved me."

"And?"

"You were at the wedding. I think you know what happened."

"But you stayed married for more than a year," I said.

She nodded. "I stayed married for longer so it looked real, and so you and Mother couldn't give me a hard time. And so that Robert would think I gave it an actual shot."

"You played the poor bastard."

Serena shrugged. "He knew what he was getting into. He went to Harvard, you know. It's not like he can claim ignorance as a defense."

I poured myself some more champagne. This lunch wasn't going how I'd planned. "Forgive *me* for being ignorant, but what does this little tragi-comedy have to do with Blake and her questionable work background?"

"At your wedding, I drank my face off and then confided in Robert. You know how when I get drunk, my stupid conscience tends to show up?"

That elicited a small smile from me. "Actually, I had no idea it ever showed up."

"Ha ha. Anyway, I told him what I'd found out about Blake. I said I was considering exposing her in order to inherit the whole trust. But then Robert said if I did, he'd go public with the whole story—about me offering to pay him to marry me."

She looked sad again, and her throat worked as she had another gulp of Veuve. "He said I deserved it—for being such a hypocrite. He even said he'd hire a legal team to keep me from my inheritance."

"Why would he get so involved?"

"He said that you looked happy, and that Blake seemed nice, and that no matter what your actual arrangement was, it was none of my business because I'd cheated the terms of the trust, too."

"That's a pretty strong stance."

Serena nodded, looking defeated. "I'm pretty sure he hates me."

"He doesn't hate you," I said. "He probably just wants to see you grow up at some point."

That sparked some interest in her eyes. "So what

exactly *did* Robert say when you talked to him last night?"

I shrugged. "Nothing."

"Don't be such a guy!" Her face regained some of its usual agitated animation. "So, why don't you think he hates me? He obviously hates me."

I sighed. "He didn't say anything specific, but he's obviously trying to keep you in line."

"I don't know why. We've been done for a long time." Serena pursed her red lips.

I couldn't believe that I had to spell this out to her. I, who had the emotional intelligence of a Neanderthal. "News flash—it means Robert hasn't totally given up on you yet, although I'm not sure why."

She appeared slightly mollified. "Oh. Huh."

"So, let's get back to the trust. I want to be clear about this. You're going after the trust provisions themselves so that you can inherit the money no matter what Robert does. And you're going to leave Blake and her situation out of it. Right?" I looked at her menacingly.

She nodded. "I won't say a word about Blake. I actually like her. I'm kind of psyched I don't have to ruin her life."

"So why don't you just let it be? Why go after the provisions at all?"

"It's a safety net," Serena said. "Robert said he

wouldn't do anything unless I contested your inheritance, but that's not good enough for me. I need a guarantee that I'm getting that money. I totally need to renovate my townhouse—it's so out of date!"

Talking about the money and renovations seemed to restore her, as did another sip of champagne. "The good news is you're in the clear. My hands are tied, so I won't say a word about Blake. And if it turns out the trust provisions are void, you don't have to stay married to her, either."

Serena watched my face, which I hoped remained impassive. "Not that you mind being married to her." She was fishing, but I didn't take the bait. I motioned to the waiter for what was surely an outrageous lunch check.

"You should know—it was nothing personal against Blake," Serena said. "She gave me some good advice about how to deal with Robert. I'm a little bummed I have to split the trust with you, but… I figure Mom would have wanted it that way."

A flutter of something I didn't recognize flashed in my chest. *Was there actual hope for my sister?* I decided to get out of there before this got too touch-feely. I rose from the table. "Keep me posted."

"Aren't you giving me a ride home?" she called.

"I think you need to walk. That bottle of champagne

was about six hundred calories."

I wasn't sure, but I thought she might have given me the finger as I left.

I stared out the car window, unseeing, as Ian brought me back to my office. I should be relieved by the conversation with Serena, but instead, I felt ill at ease. She'd basically told me that I was going to inherit my share of the trust no matter what, and that I didn't need to stay married for the rest of the year. A few short weeks ago, I would have been thrilled with the news. It would have made all the difference in the world to me, because then I wouldn't have had to pay an escort two million dollars to marry me.

But that was then. This was now.

If the trust terms were deemed voidable, I would inherit the money soon. I wouldn't have to stay married to Blake for the rest of the year. We wouldn't have to pretend to be madly in love, and I wouldn't conscientiously consummate our marriage every single night, often several times a night.

In other words, I wouldn't need her anymore. She could go.

The thought made me physically ill.

So I went home to the one person who could make it all better—the one I was also beginning to see as the root of my problem.

BLAKE

Lucas had texted me from the car to tell me he was on his way home.

He told me he wanted me in bed, ready for him.

I did as I was told, anxious to be with him. I tried to quiet that part of myself that was aching for him. I needed to get my shit together. *Because there is only one way this is ending, and that is in tears.*

But I had a whole year before I had to cry, I reminded myself. A smile played on my lips as I took a quick shower and waited for him. Even though it had only been a few short weeks, my attachment to Lucas had grown strong. I missed him when he left for work, and I couldn't wait for him to come through the door and take me into his arms at the end of the day.

I was waiting for him on the bed when he came in, his dark eyes were stormy. "Hey," I said, sitting up, "is everything okay?"

"I don't want to talk." Lucas stripped off his coat and tie and began unbuttoning his shirt.

"That bad, huh?"

I caught a brief flash of pain on his face, but it disappeared quickly. He came to me and buried his face against my chest. I ran my fingers through his thick curls, relishing the feel of his naked body on mine. But I could also feel waves of worry rolling off of him. Maybe a deal had gone sour at work.

I traced my fingers down his face and over his bottom lip. He grabbed my hand, pulling it over my head, and brought his lips against mine for a savage, consuming kiss. His erection rubbed fiercely against me, straining with need.

I was dizzy, almost breathless, by the time he finally pulled back. He leaned up, his sculpted torso above mine, and stared down at me. I knew he didn't want to talk about it, but something was definitely off. I wanted to ask if it was me, if I'd done something to upset him.

But just as I opened my mouth to ask the question, his lips were on mine, devouring me again.

Using his knee, Lucas spread my legs apart. He took both my hands and threaded his fingers through mine, then pinned them above my head. He dipped his hips, rubbing his cock back and forth against my slick heat until I was moaning, begging him to enter me.

He obeyed, penetrating me all at once, his thickness filling me completely.

I gasped at the fullness. "*Fuck,* Lucas."

His thrusts were rapid and deep. Almost desperate. He was so hard that he rubbed against that part of me only he could reach—what I assumed was my G-spot. He continued to stroke me deep inside, his thrusts relentless, punishing, and insistent. He claimed me by going deeper each time. No one else could ever love me like this. I cried out, tears running down my face, as I came so hard I saw stars.

Then he came in me, grunting and crushing me against him. My pussy quaked around him and sucked everything he had to give, pleasure and pure female triumph radiating through me. When we could finally move again, he pulled me next to him, cradled me closely against his chest, and stroked my hair. Lucas's tenderness was raw. It was real. I never felt so cared for, so *vital* to someone else, in my entire life as I did just then.

He was clutching me as if I was the last life preserver on the *Titanic.*

So I was confused when, a minute later, he jumped

up from the bed and ran for the shower so fast that it almost gave me whiplash.

THE REST of the week passed in a similar fashion. A surly Lucas would come home from work early every day, and we would make love furiously. I caught him staring at me on several occasions with a fierce, longing look in his eyes.

Finally, one night over our third respective glasses of wine, I couldn't take it anymore. "What the hell is the matter with you?" I blurted out.

He blinked in surprise. "You can tell something's bothering me?"

"It's sort of obvious. At least to me."

For some reason, that statement seemed to make him look even angrier. "That's just fucking perfect."

I wanted to ask what was so perfect that he had to describe it with the word "fucking," but I thought better of it.

"It's just some stuff at work. A deal that's gotten completely out of my control." He scrubbed a hand across his face. "I don't know what I'm going to do about it, actually."

"That doesn't sound like you," I said, trying to be encouraging.

"No, it doesn't, does it?" His tone was sharp.

I stiffened. "Are you angry at me for some reason?"

"No." His denial sounded like a lie. That didn't prevent him from pulling me onto his lap and taking me six ways from Sunday when we tumbled into bed a few minutes later.

And it didn't prevent me from screaming his name when I came so hard I was momentarily blinded.

Orgasms aside, Lucas's foul mood put me in a foul mood. And the next day, after I'd hit the gym and taken a shower, there was a clear sign that my mood wasn't going to lift anytime soon. There was a call on the house phone from the lobby. "Your sister's here to see you, Mrs. Ford."

"I'm sorry?" My voice sounded tinny, as though it was coming from far away.

"Chelsea Maxwell's here for you," the hostess said brightly. "Your sister?"

My heart was hammering in my chest. *Fucking Chelsea.* "Oh, of course! Tell her I'll be right there!" I slammed down the phone, cursing and spluttering to myself. I had to get down to the lobby fast. She might make a scene, but there was no way I was letting my crazy sister up here. She might try to hide in one of the many bedrooms, and I would never find her.

I hustled into the lobby and spotted her blond head. Her hair looked as though it had been straightened recently, stick-straight without a flyaway in sight, in spite of the humidity. *If she used my mother's prescription money for a blowout at a blow-dry bar, I swear to God...*

She spotted me and jumped to her feet. "Hey!" Chelsea pulled me in for a big, squeezy hug then released me. A Cheshire Cat grin crossed her face. "I'm so glad we're going to finally hang out!" Her voice was too loud for the lobby.

People were smiling at us. We simply looked like two sisters who were thrilled to see each other. I just wanted to wrap my fingers around her throat and squeeze and squeeze, but instead, I gave her a big, fake smile of my own. "Hang out?" I asked innocently and in a voice several decibels lower than hers. "I don't remember making plans to hang out." I grabbed her by the elbow and dragged her through the lobby, the fake smile never leaving my face.

When we got outside, Ian was unfortunately waiting. "Mrs. Ford." He nodded. "Can I take you somewhere?"

"Uh... um..."

"Absofreakinglutely!" Chelsea charged forward. "We'd like to go to The Palm."

Ian looked as if he was abstaining from raising an eyebrow. "The Palm? Of course." He held the door open for my sister, and she slid in, tossing her hair behind her and not bothering to say thank you.

"Sorry about this," I said lowly to Ian. I'd never asked him to drive me anywhere without Lucas. I walked if I needed to get somewhere.

"Don't be sorry," he said with an easy smile. "Mr. Ford'll be thrilled that you finally put me to use."

After Ian put the car in drive, Chelsea turned to me. "Does he just sit here all day and wait for you?"

I just looked at her. "He can hear you, you know."

She tossed her hair again, and I fought the urge to grab a handful of it and yank. "I didn't say anything wrong. I just think it's *cool*." She pulled out her cell phone and proceeded to take a selfie against the luxurious leather seat.

"Where are you posting that?" I asked nervously.

"Nowhere. Just Instagram. And I'm copying it to Facebook and Twitter." She looped her arm around my shoulder and took another one with me in it.

"What? *No!* I don't do social media."

"That's okay," Chelsea said, looking at the shot she'd just taken. "You have, like, five chins in this picture anyway."

"Gee, thanks." I tried to recover from her sudden

appearance by leaning back against the cool leather of the air-conditioned car. "How's Mom? Is she still congested?"

"She's *fine*." Chelsea yawned. "She's always fine." My sister had never cared about my mother's illness. It was an inconvenience for her, and she didn't have time for inconveniences. She was too busy plotting, scheming, and getting her nails done.

"She's actually not always fine." I let my eyes wander over my sister, noticing she had a new Coach purse and was wearing an expensive-looking, albeit tacky, tight-fitting rhinestone tank top. Her nails were freshly done and, as I'd already noticed, so was her hair. "Where'd you get all the fancy clothes?"

She shrugged. "Mom got me some new stuff."

"Mom?" I tensed. "How'd she do that?" I'd only sent my mother enough money for groceries, rent, and her medications. I would have sent more, but I'd feared my sister would swoop in and try to take some of Lucas's money while I was still on assignment.

"I asked her for a few new things." She ran her gel-manicured fingertips through her hair. "I figured, since our family's getting upgraded and all, I needed to look the part. It's nice, right?"

"Mom doesn't have any extra money to give you." My

panic was rising. If Chelsea had talked her out of getting her prescriptions, I was going to freak.

"I know. So she opened a new credit card and told me I could get a few things. I only spent, like, two thousand dollars."

I started coughing so hard, she had to slap me on the back.

"Mom doesn't *have* two thousand dollars—plus interest," I spluttered.

"Now that you mention it, she doesn't, really..." Chelsea cocked her eyebrow. "But you do."

I shot her a *shut-the-hell-up* look and moved as far away from her as possible. "We'll talk about that at lunch."

We pulled up at The Palm, a pricey steakhouse that Chelsea had probably heard about on *Keeping Up With the Kardashians.* "I'll be waiting for you," Ian said, nodding as he helped us out.

"I could totally get used to this," my sister said.

I groaned inwardly but re-plastered that fake smile onto my face. I wasn't going to let Chelsea trip me up. She was here for a reason, and that reason had everything to do with her new Coach purse and the two thousand dollars she'd already racked up on my poor mother's credit card. She wanted more. She was the queen of wanting—scratch that, *demanding*—something for nothing.

We were ushered inside the cool, dark restaurant and seated in a booth. Chelsea immediately ordered a glass of Chardonnay, which was promptly delivered by our suit-clad waiter. Chelsea perused the menu, looking confused. "There aren't any prices!"

I groaned. "That just means it's ridiculously expensive, and that if you're eating here, you don't need to worry about it."

She sat back, appraising me. "Well, well, well. Your Highness certainly seems to have learned a thing or two about fine living."

I bristled against her words but tried not to show it. One thing Chelsea loved to do was press my buttons. "How's Vince?" I asked. I didn't care, but I felt as though she needed to be put in her place.

She shrugged. "He's a deadbeat. I don't know what you ever saw in him."

When I'd fallen in love with Vince, he was a boy with an athletic body and a lopsided smile. He paid attention to me. He made me feel very special for a very short period of time. When he turned cold, he left me scrambling to figure out what I'd done wrong. Which, when you had Daddy issues, was sort of exactly what you thought you deserved.

"He was my high school sweetheart, remember? And then he was my fiancé? And then *you* started sleeping with him, and he broke off our engagement a month before our wedding?" I grabbed her wine and took a gulp. "And then *you* married him. Is any of this ringing a bell?"

She grabbed her wine back and rolled her eyes at me. "I can't believe you're still hanging onto that. You need to let it go—it's ancient history."

I motioned for the waiter and ordered wine. If anyone could drive me to drink, it was my sister.

"He's trying to get out of paying me alimony, saying that our marriage was so short-term, I should be ready to be 'back in the workforce,'" Chelsea continued, not missing a beat. "Can you imagine? The nerve!"

I leaned forward. "I still don't understand how you ever got alimony in the first place. You were only married for a few years. No kids. What's the basis?"

Chelsea sniffed. "He *wanted* me to quit my job and stay home. To take care of him. To make his dinner and do his laundry."

"But as soon as he asked you, you quit your job at the bank. If I remember correctly, you were thrilled about it —it's not like he asked you to give up a job you loved."

She looked as though she was going to argue, but thankfully, the waiter interrupted us by serving my wine and taking our lunch order. Chelsea ordered the Chef's three-course tasting menu—probably because she pegged it as the most expensive—and then looked at me coyly across the sleek, wooden table. "So, enough about that. You're married and all now. To a *billionaire*." She played with her wine glass. "All fancy and uppity and all. And you're wearing Christian Louboutin shoes, for Christ's sake. What's it like?"

"What's *what* like?"

The coy look evaporated. "To be rich. To live like that, in a fancy apartment with a driver and more money than you know what to do with. What's it like?"

Chelsea had been hustling since the day she'd been born. She'd always wanted to live the high life; she had champagne tastes on a Miller Lite budget. When Vince had proved to be more talk than delivery in the earnings department, she had promptly divorced him. She'd been looking for Mr. Right-and-Rich ever since, and not necessarily in that order.

"The lifestyle's nice, but it's ridiculous. When you think about how *we* live—just over the bridge in our crappy apartments, it seems opulent. When you think about how people all over the *world* live—in shanty-towns, without running water or electricity—it's too much. But Lucas gives a ton of money to charity. He's wealthy because he's brilliant and he's worked hard his entire life. He doesn't even seem to care about material things."

My sister snorted. "That sounds like one of those actresses—like Kristen Stewart—who says they don't care about being famous, but they are *so* famous. That's a problem I'd like to have. I care about material things. I just wish I had more of them to care about."

"Then you should try getting a job." With all the effort she put into getting something for nothing, it was like a full-time job anyway.

"I'm thinking about going back to school." She dove into her appetizer of bacon-wrapped scallops and moaned, fluttering her eyelids. "These are so good." She didn't offer me any.

"You mean to get your GED?"

"I graduated from high school," she snapped.

"Barely."

She leaned across the table and glared at me. "For a hooker, you seriously have a superiority complex."

"Please keep your voice down," I begged.

"You need to stop acting like you're better than the rest of us."

"I don't think I'm better than anybody else." I picked at my wedge salad, wishing we were finished and I could get the hell away from her. "So... school for what?" I hated to ask, but this was the portion of the program where Chelsea finally got to the point. I motioned to the waiter for more wine, because I felt certain it was going to be a doozy.

"Acting school. There's this really great one in New York that I want to apply to." My sister's eyes glittered with excitement.

"I didn't know you wanted to be an actress." *I thought you just wanted to be a diva, with a driver, Louis Vuitton luggage, and a pair of big-ass sunglasses. On your Miller-Lite budget.*

"I'm thinking about trying out for *The Bachelorette.*" She tossed her hair. "You don't have to be an actress to get on there, but I bet it helps. I would kill it on that show. I'm totally perfect for it."

I opened my mouth and then closed it. Chelsea, queen of looking good for no reason, constant scheming and zero loyalty, would *totally* kill it on *The Bachelorette.*

The idea of my sister relocating for school was immediately appealing, until it sank in that someone was going to have to fund her Manhattan lifestyle—me. "That sounds exciting, but isn't it expensive? I know school's pricey, anyway, but the cost of living in New York is crazy high." I knew this because Elena had looked into expanding AccommoDating into the New York market. She'd said the higher prices we could charge wouldn't offset the price for office space, which she called "completely fucking exorbitant."

Last time I checked, completely fucking exorbitant wasn't in my sister's budget.

"Tuition's about one hundred thousand dollars. And I'll need living expenses and money for clothes, of course." Chelsea casually adjusted her sparkly tank top. "You can't dress like a hick in New York."

"Wow. That's a lot of money. Vince is going to need to pony up on the alimony payments."

"Vince isn't going to pay for it, silly! What he gives me is, like, coffee money compared to what I'll need." She grinned and my stomach sank. "The money's going to come from *you*. You're the only one I know who has any!"

I shook my head. "I don't have any money, though. Lucas has all the money, and I'm not asking him for a hundred thousand dollars to send you to acting school just so you can have a rose ceremony on *ABC*."

"But you have to ask him!" she said a little too brightly.

"Why?"

Chelsea leaned forward, her grin becoming triumphant. "Because if you don't, I'm going to tell his family and the press and anybody else who'll listen to me that you're a *hooker.* That before he picked you up and dusted you off, you were *literally* a filthy whore."

I recoiled from her words and the venom in her voice. "What did I ever do to you?" I didn't know why she hated me so much. First, she'd stolen Vince. Now, she was trying to ruin me so she could afford to keep herself in gel manicures and Jimmy Choos as she stalked around Manhattan, hoping to meet her near-future husband on the reality television circuit.

She didn't even blink. "You think you're better than me."

"You stole my fiancé, and you just threatened to blackmail me. I *am* better than you."

She arched an eyebrow. "See? It's that. Right there."

"*What?*"

"That holier-than-thou routine. You think you're the only one who cares about Mom. You think I'm a lazy, no-good fiancé-stealer. And you're prettier than me—not that you *think* you're prettier than me; you just *are* prettier than me. People like you better than me. It's annoying. It's tired. And now you're married to a hot billionaire, and it's not *fair.*" She sounded like a petulant teenager about to have a temper tantrum at the mall. "Mom didn't tell me anything, but I know you married him as a job. *I just know it.* So, you cough up the cash, or I'm going to cause you a world of hurt."

I looked at her defiantly. "No."

"What did you just say?"

"I just said *no*. You're not getting a dime from my hot billionaire husband. Go ask your sloppy seconds of an ex for money."

Chelsea pointed her finger at me. "You're going to regret this."

"Not as much as I'd regret funding your lifestyle and unleashing you on a bunch of poor, unsuspecting bachelors."

She picked up her fork and started eating her expensive lunch, her eyes never leaving mine. "We'll see about that."

LUCAS

"What are you saying exactly?"

Blake looked at me miserably. "I'm saying that my sister's trying to blackmail me by outing me as an escort to I don't know who—your family, the press, anyone who'll listen."

"This is your sister who stole your fiancé?"

Blake looked pale. "The one and only."

My heart ached for her. "She makes Serena look good. Not an easy task."

"I know." She sank down on the couch. "I shouldn't have taken this job. I know my sister, what she's capable of. She was born to blackmail me in a situation like this. I'm so sorry." Her voice was wobbly.

Christ. Since my lunch with Serena, I'd been trying to keep Blake at a distance, except when I was plundering her with my dick. But I couldn't bear to see her hurting. I sat down and pulled her into my arms. "We'll deal with your sister. Don't even worry about it."

Blake was stiff against me, taking no comfort in the embrace. "I don't want to give her anything."

I ran my hands down her hair. "You don't have to. I'll take care of it."

She pulled back, eyes flashing. All traces of forthcoming tears had vanished. "Lucas Ford, don't you dare!"

I blinked at her. No one had said "don't you dare" to me since my mother had caught me sneaking the gin out of the liquor cabinet when I was sixteen years old. "I don't understand why you're upset. I'm offering to make the problem go away."

"She's not just a problem—she's my *sister*, and she's a pain in the ass!" Blake's face now had two hectic spots of color on it. "If you give in to her, you'll never get rid of her. This tuition and her wannabe-New-York-City-socialite lifestyle are just the tip of the iceberg."

"There's no reason to let her upset you."

Blake threw up her hands. "There's every reason in the world for her to upset me! She's a scheming, money-grubbing, lazy you-know-what that rhymes with *blunt*!"

"So let me take care of it like I'm offering to." I tried to keep my voice gentle, but I was becoming annoyed. This was something I could fix. Even though Blake's sister didn't deserve anything, it was better to throw some money at the problem and keep her the hell away from my wife.

Blake stood up. "You can't just 'take care of it.' First of all, Chelsea's not an 'it'; she's a person! And you have to *deal* with people! You can't just throw money at everything all the time and then swagger back to your ivory tower, acting like you've solved the world's problems!"

I sat back. "I don't act like that."

She crossed her arms and raised an eyebrow. "You bought a *wife*. So that you could keep your sister from inheriting your entire family fortune, in order to give money to worthy charities *and* to piss her off in the meantime. And now you want to pay off *my* sister to make her go away, so that I don't have to be bothered by her. Are you seeing a pattern here?"

"No." I could hear the defensiveness in my voice.

"You would rather deal with dollars than people."

I got up and headed for the bourbon. "I don't see why you have to make it sound like a negative personality trait."

Blake took a step toward me. "It's only negative if it isolates you. If it keeps you from having a connection with people. If it makes you forget what's real."

I poured two fingers of the amber liquid then, after a

slight pause, made it three. "I'm all too familiar with what's real." *My mother. Elizabeth. You...*

"That's why you don't date. That's why you've never had a girlfriend since Elizabeth left you. That's why you hired me to live with you for a year—so you can give me money and send me on my way, without having to get attached!" Her whole face was flushed now, her hands clenched into tight fists.

I set the bourbon down without drinking it. "And you're so different?"

She looked slightly abashed. "I'm still close to people. And I'm not the one…"

"What?"

Blake shook her head. "Nothing. Never mind. I need to remember my place. I'm the hired help."

Her words cut me. "Don't say that."

She looked at me, her chin jutting out in an almost imperceptible sign of defiance. "The truth hurts, but don't worry. It hurts me, too." She headed down the hall. "Is it okay if I go to the gym and then take a shower? Today's sort of thrown me for a loop."

My shoulders sagged. "You don't need my permission. I'm not your jailer."

She stopped and turned to me. "So then, would you like to come with me? You've been so worried about that deal..." Her tone turned from angry to wistful. "We haven't hung out in a while."

"I have to go back to work," I said, hating myself.

The flash of disappointment across her features was clear. "Of course."

"I'll see you later, though." I wanted nothing more than to be with Blake right now. I could probably retire and just spend the rest of my years being her gym buddy, letting her order for me, and worshipping her body, not necessarily in that order. But this had to stop. She was leaving in a few months. In fact, if Serena had the trust terms annulled, Blake was leaving any second. I had to get a motherfucking grip before I let what I was feeling inside rip me apart.

Nodding, she disappeared into the bedroom.

I WAS in a foul mood at the office. Shirley tried to ask me a few questions about our new HR initiative, but I practically ripped her head off and bowled it down the hall. In an effort to calm down, I downloaded all my quarterly reports and started analyzing them. My business holdings were performing better than expected. Normally, this would satisfy me, but I couldn't keep my mind off of Blake. She'd been reeling from what her sister had pulled, yet I'd pushed her away again.

I stood up and grabbed my cell phone. I needed to go back home and make this right.

The receptionist buzzed in. "Mr. Ford, there's someone here to see you."

"I don't have any appointments," I snapped. I never had any appointments. I made Shirley do all my dirty work, and I paid her quite handsomely for it.

Another example of throwing money at your problems, my inner analyst chimed in.

Fuck off, I chimed back.

"It's Chelsea Maxwell."

"I see." *The sister has balls. Time to cut them off.* "Bring her in."

My receptionist appeared shortly thereafter, followed by a young woman who looked strikingly similar to Blake. She had long blond hair and blue eyes, but she was slightly shorter and curvier. Where Blake's skin was smooth and fair, Chelsea's was a deep bronze, as though she spent a fair amount of time at M Street Beach with a big bottle of coconut-scented oil, a stash of wine coolers, and a red Solo cup at her side.

Her ample assets almost burst out of her black, low-cut dress that seemed to have a death grip on her body.

Spiked heels, big hoop earrings, and lots of black mascara completed the look—a Southie hottie in her prime, out for an afternoon stroll, an iced coffee with extra cream from Dunkin' Donuts, and a side of blackmail.

Someone had left Blake for *her*? I couldn't fathom it. But then again, Elizabeth had left me for my father, who favored ascots and wore argyle socks to bed. People were so fucking weird. That was why hiding in my office was awesome.

Not that I was actually admitting to that.

The receptionist closed the door behind her, and Chelsea batted her dangerously long lashes at me. "Lucas Ford, we finally meet! It's such a pleasure."

She held out her hand to shake mine, but I just motioned for her to sit. "What do you want, Chelsea?"

She pouted a little, her pillowy lips forming an annoyed O. "So formal! We're family now. You can relax." She positioned herself in her chair so that her breasts were jutting toward me. "I finally saw Blake. She seems like she's doing well."

"Really? She didn't mention it," I lied.

Chelsea sniffed. "She wouldn't, would she? Mom and I didn't even get invited to the wedding."

"I think you know the reason for that."

She peeked up at me from under her lashes, and I

wanted to smack her. "You mean..."—she leaned forward—"because she's a... *you know?*"

"Episcopalian?"

Chelsea cocked her head, looking confused. "Huh?"

Not as pretty as Blake, and nowhere near as smart. "Never mind. You were saying?"

"I was saying that we didn't get invited to your wedding because my sister's a hooker, and you didn't want your family to know." She appeared satisfied with herself.

"Ah." I sat back in my chair. "That."

Chelsea sat there, waiting for me to say more, or at least look surprised. "Yeah," she finally said, "*that.*"

I shrugged. "What about it?"

"You tell me," she said, her voice provocative.

"You called this meeting, Chelsea. I have no idea why you're here."

The smug look slid off of her face. "The hell you don't."

"Ah, I see your true colors run close to the surface," I said. "I appreciate that."

"Good." Her tone was all business now. "I told Blake today—I need money for school and to relocate to New York. She said she wouldn't give me anything, but she's holding a grudge against me for some old stuff. She wouldn't even consider it. She's not thinking clearly."

"What do you mean by 'old stuff'? The fact that you stole her fiancé a month before her wedding, and that you married him yourself?"

Undeterred, she looked at me coyly. "If you met Vince, you'd know I did her a favor. I helped her dodge a bullet."

I gave her a tight smile. "How very philanthropic of you."

She looked confused again but quickly shook it off. "Whatever. I need money to start my new life. I'm coming to you because you're the only person in our family who can help."

"I'm not in the business of giving handouts."

Her throat worked as she swallowed. "I'm not looking for a *handout*. You do something for me; I do something for you."

I leaned forward. "And what's that?"

Taking my stance as a cue, she also leaned forward. Her breasts seemed dangerously close to popping out of her dress. "That all depends on what you want, big boy. Some people like to call it a sister act. You get what you have with Blake, and you get me on the side." She lowered her voice conspiratorially. "I'm told that I'm a little spicier than my sister. She might be better-looking, but I can give you what you really want."

"I don't think you can."

She licked her lips and my skin crawled. "Lemme give it a try."

"Blake was right." I smiled at her again, sitting back against my seat. "You really are a piece of work. But you were sort of right, too."

She cocked an eyebrow, still looking hopeful.

"Your sister's *much* better-looking than you. She's also kind, thoughtful, intelligent, and altogether in another class of human beings. I wouldn't touch you with a ten-foot pole wrapped in Clorox wipes."

She straightened, her cheeks heated. "Suit yourself."

"Are we done?"

"Not quite." She pursed her lips and adjusted the top of her dress, putting her boobs away. "I can always go to the press about my sister and her questionable work history. Or your dad. Or your work partners. Or whoever will listen to me. I'd gladly take money in exchange for my silence."

"Done," I said.

Chelsea looked stunned. "Really?"

"Really."

"What's the catch?"

"You'll have to sign an airtight confidentiality agreement and a contract with me," I said. "This is a one and done, Chelsea. I give you this money, and you agree to walk away forever. You can't come back and ask me for more, because there won't be any. And you have to leave Blake alone for good. No more threats. Understand?"

She nodded, her eyes glittering. "How much money?"

"More, much more than you deserve. Enough to pay your tuition and get you settled in New York. Enough to keep you comfortable for years to come, provided you don't blow it. But if you contact the press or take any other steps to harm your sister, I'm coming after you with an army of attorneys. We'll take your money and whatever possessions you have and leave you on the street—literally. Sound fair?"

She nodded quickly, as if she were afraid I would change my mind. "S-sure."

"Fine. Wait in the next room. I'll have my attorney prepare the documents right now. You'll be on your way with a check before the close of business."

She opened her mouth and then, thankfully, closed it. I buzzed Shirley and had Chelsea removed to a waiting room far from my sight. Sister act, indeed.

Then I called my attorney and started the process to have Blake's leech of a sister removed from her side. Forever.

BLAKE

Running on the treadmill helped clear my head. Afterward, as I stood underneath the hot water from the shower, I realized what I needed to do: just be there for Lucas. He'd been tense for the last few weeks, struggling with work, then I'd gone and thrown the episode with my sister at him.

He'd only been trying to help. What he maybe didn't understand was that I'd wanted him to just hold me, let me complain about Chelsea, and stroke my hair. I'd wanted him to go to the gym with me and let me rail against my sister some more. I'd wanted him to act like my husband—a normal, mere mortal one—not an alpha CEO billionaire fixer of all things.

But that was exactly who he was.

What I'd said to him about his personality was what I

believed to be the truth. It was also completely inappropriate for me to have spoken to him like that. He was my fake husband, not my real one. I would do well to remember that. I'd found myself staring at the way my engagement ring sparkled in the sunlight one too many times lately, and I'd been inhaling his scent from the T-shirts he tossed casually on the floor of our room. I'd caught myself wondering what it would be like if this assignment could last forever.

But Lucas was my client, and it was my job to make him happy. So I quickly dried off, braided my hair, and threw on a dress. I decided to head to his office to say that I was sorry about my rogue mouth, and to see if he could sneak out to have dinner with me in the North End. Maybe we could even go back to *Mio Fratello* and have that olive-and-pasta appetizer.

I might even share with him.

Ian pulled up outside of Lucas's building in the Financial District. "I'll circle the block until you text me." He shot me a grin and rolled the window up, waiting until I was safely on the sidewalk before merging back into the light evening traffic. Ian had seemed a lot happier since we'd abandoned my sister at The Palm this afternoon.

Hope lit up my heart as I went into the lobby. Even though I knew the truth about our relationship, I still got a little thrill when I was about to see my handsome husband. But that thrill turned into a near heart attack as the elevator doors opened and Chelsea exited them.

She sashayed across the lobby and my jaw dropped.

I jumped back against a dark-paneled wall and hid behind a potted tree so she couldn't see me. *What the hell?* She was wearing a skin-tight dress and the pushiest of all push-up bras. She was also wearing a cat-that-just-ate-the-canary smile, and had a little extra jiggle in her step that made me cringe.

What was she doing there?

My stomach plummeted as I ran through the options. She was here to ask Lucas for money. She was here to hit on Lucas. She was here to ask Lucas for money *and* hit on him. Whatever it was, she had gotten what she wanted. I could tell that much from her saucy walk as she passed through the revolving doors.

Lucas had given her what she wanted without asking me. And whether that was money, attention, or something even worse—he had broken my trust.

I hadn't even realized that I'd trusted him until that point.

Waiting until my sister was gone, I hustled out to the street. I had to get away from him. And Chelsea. And whatever it was that had sprung up between them.

IT'S NOT that I was drunk, exactly, but I had just finished an entire bottle of wine. Then I'd just about finished another one. I sat on the bed in my hotel room, drinking straight out of the bottle and watching HBO. Unfortunately, *Pretty Woman* was on, and I couldn't make myself turn it off.

I refused to think about the pretty escort and her handsome billionaire client, but the images still captivated me. That was the problem with being drunk. You couldn't stop watching *Pretty* Woman even though it hit too close to home. You couldn't make yourself do what you should—stop drinking. And you couldn't control your thoughts so you would stop thinking about a certain someone—your hot billionaire husband who'd hired you to be his fake wife. And who was quite possibly cheating on you with your sister.

Or something. Maybe.

I tried to shake that thought off, but I was up to my esophagus with wine. Shaking or moving anything at all seemed like an Olympian feat right now.

The image of my sister in the lobby haunted me—her jiggling boobs, her perfect ass, her insidiously glinting hoop earrings. My thoughts drifted back to that night, years before, when I'd found my sister in bed with

Vince. *Did I forget to mention that part, Lucas? That I found them together? In my own goddamned bed?* Even the voice in my head was slurring.

I tried to block out the images, but my mind—ugly with wine—refused to cooperate.

I turned back to the movie, trying to concentrate. A few minutes later, I realized I was crying, and I was too drunk to stop.

Julia Roberts was trying on dresses with the nice woman who knew Richard Gere wasn't her uncle.

Vince's white ass is pumping his dick into a woman on all fours in front of him, and he's giving it to her much harder than he ever gives it to me.

Julia was trying to eat an escargot but instead, flung it across the room.

I can see the woman's hair as she tosses her head back and lets out a deep, guttural moan. Her hair is long and blond, just like mine. I wonder if I'm having an out-of-body experience and that's actually me on the bed. But then Vince grabs her hair and yanks it, a litany of curses streaming out of his mouth. He says that no one makes him come this hard; no one else can do it.

It's not my hair he's grabbing.

Julia Roberts was taking a bath with a Walkman on, adorably singing along to Prince. Richard Gere was sitting on the edge of the tub, watching her.

And she orders him to do it harder, because he's the only one who can make her come like this, too. Then I walk into the room a little farther, and I realize it's my sister. Vince is fucking my sister, and he's so busy having an orgasm and fingering her clit—which I have to do for myself when we have sex—that he doesn't even see me standing there. But my sister does. My sister does, and she doesn't stop him.

Richard placed the stunning necklace on Julia and then took her to the opera.

Vince and Chelsea elope in Jamaica. She comes back and spreads the pictures all over my mother's coffee table—pictures of the two of them, smiling and tan, with palm trees and sparkling aqua water all around them.

Julia and Richard were at the polo match, where he saw her with another man and felt a stab of jealousy.

Chelsea is leaving Lucas's office today, looking like the cat that just swallowed the canary.

Chelsea would love to screw my handsome billionaire husband's brains out, because that's what she did. She stole things from me. Maybe it made her orgasms better, like those people who enjoyed choking themselves during sex or the ones who liked to be tied up. It heightened the sensation or something.

But he wouldn't touch her. Lucas wouldn't do that to me, and I knew it.

Of course, I'd said the same thing about Vince.

LUCAS

"What the hell do you mean, you don't know where she went?" I practically spit the words out at Ian.

"I dropped her at your office at seven. I told her I'd circle the block until she texted. She said you two were going to dinner in the North End."

"She never told me she was coming. She never even came up." My heart was pounding in my chest, quite possibly skipping beats. "You didn't see her leave?"

"No sir. I was driving around the block, but there was traffic over on Congress." Ian's throat worked as he swallowed.

I tried to call Blake, but it didn't even ring. It went straight to voice mail. "They haven't seen her at The Stratum. No one's come or gone from the penthouse since she left earlier tonight. And there's been no activity on any of the credit cards she has."

"Did you call the police?" Ian asked.

"Not yet. I think there's something else going on." I pinched the bridge of my nose. Maybe Chelsea had immediately called her. Chelsea could have ignored our agreement and told Blake that I'd given her five million dollars, and Blake was beside-herself angry with me.

Maybe Blake had run into her sister here at my building, and Chelsea had told her. Or maybe Blake had just seen her sister leaving and drawn her own conclusions.

"I'll walk home," I told Ian.

"Sir?"

"Jesus Christ, it's not that far," I snapped. "If you hear from her, call me immediately."

I fumed as I walked from my office through Downtown Crossing, past Suffolk Law School, and into the park. It was quiet at this hour, with the swan boats closed and the screaming children stuffed back into their minivans and driven home to whichever suburb they were from. I stalked down the path, not even seeing the trees around me, their limbs heavy with fragrant blooms.

"Hey!" a familiar voice shouted. I stopped, confused,

until I realized that it was Herman Pace. I'd practically walked right past him.

I stopped. "Hey."

"What's your problem? And don't say nothing because you look like you just took a bite of moldy cheese."

I shrugged. "Work stuff. Nothing I can't handle."

"How's that beautiful wife of yours?" he asked.

"She's turning out to be somewhat of a disappointment."

He sat up straighter. "Why's that?"

"It's complicated." *I have feelings for her and it's totally f'd up. I can't even deal with it.*

He shook his head and rolled his eyes. "That's the problem with you rich people—the same thing that's wrong with celebrities. Can't be happy with what you've got. Everything's too *complicated*. Or it's not *perfect*. You all are getting married and divorced and remarried faster than the rest of us can keep track of."

"Really?" I asked. "You're keeping track of celebrity marriages these days?"

"People throw those magazines away in the trash every day—which is where they belong. But I can't help it if I get sucked into the headlines." He adjusted his wool hat, which he wore every night, even in the summer. "How'd she disappoint you?"

I groaned. "I really don't want to talk about it. I need to think it through."

"Well, go on and do that. But don't make a woman like that wait too long. She might not stick around."

I bristled at the thought. "Are you talking from experience?"

"I learned the hard way." He motioned me on. "Let me be a lesson to you."

Confused anger thrummed through me as I headed home. I stopped in the bar at The Stratum, which I never did, but I couldn't bear to go upstairs yet. I ordered a Manhattan and nursed it, not even seeing the people around me. Blake must've seen her sister at my office, and she must've thought the worst. And now she was gone.

Even since Elizabeth had left me, and involved me in an ugly personal scandal, I'd chosen to live my life alone. And it had been fine, almost perfect, until Blake had shown up… My phone buzzed, and I picked it up without even looking at the number. It had to be her.

"Lucas?" It was my sister, Serena.

"What?" I snapped.

"I just got off the phone with my attorney. He said that based on his team's research, he believes the social provisions in our trust are voidable. He's putting together a brief and calling Rupert first thing in the morning."

"That's just fucking perfect." I finished my Manhattan in one gulp.

"What's *your* problem?" she asked, but I hung up before giving her an answer.

My problem? Blake left me tonight, and I don't know where she is.

She left me because she thought I'd gone behind her back and done something with Sister Act.

She didn't give me a chance to explain myself.

And now I don't have to stay married to her for the rest of the year, because I can inherit the money anyway.

There was an acrid taste in my mouth that I knew was not just from the alcohol. I was going to have to tell her the truth, and soon—so that she could go. I motioned for the bartender. The thought literally drove me to drink.

As a venture capitalist, I took pride in always telling myself the truth. I assessed corporations' strengths and weaknesses, ruthlessly ascertaining the value of their technology. Before I made a major investment, I asked myself a series of questions: Was the technology a market disruptor? Could it capture a significant share of the market? Was it solving a must-have need?

There were other considerations, but these were the

most important. I wanted wow-factor technology. Anything less didn't hold my interest. I guess the same was true in my personal life. I wasn't interested in pursuing a relationship just for the sake of having one.

To me, Blake was the equivalent of a massive market disruptor. She'd captured more than a significant share of the market—she'd captured the *whole* market. She was solving a must-have need, a need I hadn't even known existed in my pre-Blake world.

For fuck's sake. I was in love with her, and it was never going to work. She could have talked to me tonight. She could've asked me about Chelsea. Instead, she ran.

Bitter disappointment coursed through me as I considered what she must be thinking: That I'd let her down. That she couldn't trust me. That I'd gone behind her back.

Well, I *had* gone behind her back, but it was to protect her. If I hadn't taken care of Chelsea right then and there, she'd be setting up a press conference and plastering pictures of Blake and me all over social media. Instead, she was on her way to pack for New York. She was going to leave Boston, and she was going to leave us alone.

Us. Who was I kidding? Blake had run away from me without a word. She hadn't even given me the opportunity to explain myself, or defend myself, or even say good-bye.

Christ. Was I saying good-bye to her now?

I grabbed my next Manhattan and proceeded to drown my sorrows. I would say good-bye to her tomorrow. Tonight, I was getting shit-faced.

BLAKE

After I took two ibuprofen, I texted my mother to let her know I was on my way. She just texted back a question mark. I wasn't sure what I was going to tell her.

My stomach sank as my cab drove into the section of Southie where we lived. South Boston had become home to many young professionals over the past decade, but there was no gentrification in our neighborhood. Faded baby-blue paint peeled in rolls from the exterior of our multi-family building. Weeds grew out of the cracks in the sidewalk out front, and empty cans of *Schlitz* littered our shared porch.

Home sweet home. I'd always hated it there, but it was worse now because I knew I was never getting out.

My mother was sitting on the couch, wrapped in an

old afghan, with a bunch of crumpled tissues next to her.

I hugged her, pulling her close. "What's the matter?"

"Like you don't know." Her voice was wobbly.

I knelt down and grabbed her hands. "Know what?"

She pursed her lips, but her accusatory look faded, replaced by unshed tears. "You don't know about your sister?"

The headache from my hangover started to pound worse. "Is she okay?"

My mother grabbed another tissue and blew her nose loudly. "She's leaving town. Moving to New York, of all places. She's probably going to become a Yankees fan. I don't know where I went wrong with that girl. I tried to raise her right."

I sank down onto the couch next to her. "She's really going?"

My mother blew her nose again. "Yes. She said she ran into some good luck and finally had the money to move. She's going to acting school." She turned and looked at me. "I don't know where all this money came from. I didn't want to tell you this, but I'd lent her some money a couple of weeks ago. Actually, I opened a new credit card so she could get herself some things."

I stiffened. "You shouldn't have done that. You'll never get the money back."

My mother shook her head. "That's the crazy thing—she paid me back last night."

"Huh?" My sister never paid anyone back. Not ever.

"You heard me. She paid me back two thousand dollars. In cash. And she wasn't even bothered by it." A suspicious look was back on my mom's face. "Did you do this? Did you give her the money to go away? I know she drives you crazy, and I wouldn't even blame you after what she did with Vince—"

"It wasn't me." I swallowed hard. "It was probably Lucas."

I could feel my mother staring at me. She was probably taking in my puffy eyes and the mascara still smudged on my face, that I hadn't bothered to wash off. "Speaking of Lucas, where is he? And whad're you doing here? I thought you weren't coming back until next summer."

I grabbed a tissue from her. "Can we not, please? Talk about him? Or anything to do with him?"

"Did he do something bad?"

"Yes." I blew my nose. "No. I don't know."

"Did he *hurt* you?"

"No," I said quickly. "He wouldn't do anything like that. He's not like that."

"Why would he give Chelsea money?" Her tone was

now gentle, which pushed me dangerously close to tears.

"I don't k-know." My breath hitched. "It might be because she threatened to blackmail me. Or maybe she... did something for him." I wiped roughly at my tears. I didn't want to be crying, and I didn't want to be having this conversation.

"She tried to *blackmail* you?" My mother put her hand over her heart, as if I was finally doing her in.

I nodded. "She said if I didn't give her the money to go to New York, she was going to tell everybody that I'm an escort. If that happened, Lucas would lose his trust, which is worth billions of dollars."

"Just because you have to expect the worst from your sister doesn't mean you have to expect the worst from Lucas." She patted my hair. "Then *that's* why he gave her money, sweetie. Not because of whatever else you're worrying about."

I wanted to believe that was true. But that want—that piercing, yearning want—didn't make it true. "But I told him not to. I know she's your daughter, and she's my sister, but she's a Grade-A leech, Mom. If he gives her money, she'll never go away."

"Except that she's packing up to leave and do just that."

It seemed too good to be true, but I didn't want to say that to her.

"I saw her coming out of his office." My voice was low and hoarse. "She was wearing this skin-tight black dress. She strutted through the lobby like she owned it."

My mother put her arm around me. "Your sister always walks like that. She walks through Target like that. It doesn't mean Lucas did anything with her."

"Vince did."

"Vince is an idiot, and you know it."

I started crying, but then I laughed. "Vince *is* an idiot, and I *do* know it."

"Lucas shouldn't have to pay for what's happened in your past." Her voice was gentle again.

I shook my head. "You're right. He shouldn't. But it doesn't matter. What happened in my past has nothing to do with him. We don't have a future, anyway. He's my client." I wrapped my arms around myself, feeling as though I was physically wounded.

My mother looked at me and frowned. "If he's your client, and you're still on assignment, why are you home, crying into my afghan?"

I blew my nose again. "I'm not."

"Um, that's my Kleenex you're blowing your nose into. So yes, you are."

"Here. Take it back." I tried to hand her my rumpled tissue, and she swatted my hand away.

"Gross! You stop that right now, young lady!"

Then we were both laughing, then she hugged me, and then I started crying again. My mother patted my back. "Why don't you go back to bed for a little while, honey? I'll make you breakfast. I bet you'll feel a lot better after that."

I nodded and headed to my room, but I knew that sleep and food wouldn't make me better. Nothing could. I slid underneath my covers and looked out at the miserable view of the yellowing multi-family unit next door. I would call Lucas after breakfast. I would tell him I hadn't been feeling well the night before and that I'd gone home so I didn't get him sick. I would live with him for the rest of the year, per the terms of our contract. I would sleep in his bed, make love to him, and do whatever he asked.

But I wasn't going to let myself feel for him anymore. I couldn't. Last night had made it very clear to me—I had real feelings for my client, and no matter how much money he gave me, I couldn't afford them. I had to say good-bye to him today, at least in my heart. Otherwise, saying good-bye to him months from now would probably kill me.

I tried to sleep, but I kept thinking about him. I

thought about the way his eyes had sparkled at our wedding, how he had carried me over the threshold, the first time we'd made love, and my world had been rocked forever.

I remembered the way he'd held me after I had a panic attack over that stupid barracuda. It was as though I was his most precious jewel, his favorite blanket, and the next technology app that was going to storm the market, all rolled into one. He wouldn't let me go. I'd felt something from him then… something real.

But I'd been fooling myself. Even if I *had* felt something from him, it was better this way. Nothing was ever going to happen between us in the long run. I was a hooker, and he was a billionaire technology magnate. He had hired me to solve a problem, because that was how he dealt with his problems, by paying them to go away.

Just like he'd done with my sister.

I would go back and perform my fake wifely duties in just a little while. For the moment, I let myself clutch my sides and cry.

LUCAS

My phone was ringing. Still in a foul mood and facing a nasty hangover, I took it from my nightstand and threw it across the room. *Fuck off.*

But then I sat up straight, because it could be *her*.

I found my phone and glared at it. The missed call was from Rupert Granger. I stalked out to the empty, quiet kitchen, made myself a coffee, and called him back. "Serena already called me," I said as a greeting.

"Jesus, she's fast," he said. "I wanted you to know that I'll be reviewing her attorney's research with my legal team. If I get the go-ahead from them, I'll be releasing the funds by the end of the week."

I felt hollowed out by the news. "That's fast."

"I know. I'll be happy to put my administrative duties to rest. Your sister's been driving me crazy about this."

I grabbed some Advil to go with my coffee. "She does that. A lot."

"I'll be in touch."

As soon as we hung up, my phone buzzed again. It was Elizabeth. I had no desire to talk to her, but I was immediately worried that something had happened to my father.

"Is everything okay?"

"Of course," she said smoothly. She sounded way too friendly for eight o'clock in the morning.

"Then why are you calling me?"

"Serena called last night. She told us about the trust. I wanted to call and say congratulations." Her tone was friendlier than it had been in years.

"Is my father there?"

"No. He's already at the club." Her voice was husky. "Are you in the office?"

"Not yet."

"How're things going with Blake?" she asked.

"Great," I lied. "Why the fuck are you asking?"

"Because I was just thinking... wouldn't it be fun if we had a little, you know... reunion?" Her tone was hot.

Of all the goddamned nerve. "Seriously?"

"Seriously." She sounded so turned on. I could just picture her running her hands over her breasts. "It would be *naughty*. You're married now; I'm married—to your *father*. You're a newly minted multi-billionaire..."

Between Chelsea and Elizabeth, I was in proposition-central station. *Jesus, they were really coming out of the woodwork.*

But I'd dealt with Chelsea. Maybe it was *finally* time to deal with Elizabeth.

"That sounds... that sounds naughty, Elizabeth. Really naughty." My tone was encouraging.

"You know I like it naughty. I promise I won't disappoint you. I never did before, did I?"

"Never," I lied agreeably. "I'd love to meet. Let's plan on this afternoon at the Four Seasons. I'll check in under a fake name—I'll text it to you later. In the meantime, to get primed, I want you to send me some pictures of you. Some *nasty* ones. You sound riled up right now. Go to your bed and take your clothes off. Pleasure yourself and take pictures. Send them to me. I want you to think of me while you're taking those pictures, baby, because I'll be thinking of you. I'm going to give it to you good and hard this afternoon. It's been too long."

"I can't wait." Her voice was breathy.

Me neither, you douche. "See you later."

I called Ian as soon as I hung up with Elizabeth. "I need you to take me to South Boston. I'll be down in ten minutes. And this afternoon, I need you to do me another favor."

ELENA ALMOST REFUSED to give me Blake's home address. True to form, I offered her an outrageous sum of money so that she would break her own confidentiality agreement and tell me where Blake lived.

Blake wouldn't approve, but also true to form, I was doing this for her own good.

And mine. Since I didn't know what she was thinking, maybe it was *just* mine.

Ian pulled up outside of a seedy-looking row house in a crumbling neighborhood. *Christ.* My wife and her mother couldn't live like this. Why didn't she tell me things were this bad?

I hit the buzzer, but there was no answer. Then I heard a voice from a window on the second floor. "What do you want?"

I looked up and saw an older, pretty woman who must have been Blake's mom. "I'm looking for Blake. It's Lucas Ford. Can I come up?"

"Hold on," she said. "I'll buzz you in."

The buzzer rang, and I went up the stairs, ignoring the stuffiness and the lingering smell of kimchi, which seemed incongruous at this hour of the morning. Blake's mother opened the door, tightening her lavender bathrobe around her. "Mrs. Maxwell. It's a pleasure. I'm sorry to come barging in first thing this morning."

"It's okay." She smiled at me and motioned me inside. "Have a seat. Would you like some coffee?"

"Sure." I sat down on the sagging couch, which was dotted with threadbare pillows.

"I'm sure our place isn't what you're used to," she called from the tiny kitchen.

Three potted violets sat on the windowsill, cutting through the dankness with some cheer.

"Your house is a lot cozier than mine. More personal touches." I accepted the coffee from her. "Is your daughter here? I need to speak with her."

She nodded and adjusted her robe again. "She's here, but I think she's pretty upset."

I set down the coffee. "I'm sure she is. I've been sort of a jerk."

Mrs. Maxwell crossed her arms against her chest. "Are you here for business?" She studied my face.

"Not if your daughter forgives me."

She smiled at me a little, looking pleased. "In that case, I will get her. And then I'll give you two some privacy. It was nice to meet you, though."

"The pleasure was mine." I bounced my knee nervously as I waited for Blake. I didn't know what I was going to say, but whatever it was, it had to be right, and it had to be fast.

Like Herman had said, a woman like Blake wasn't going to wait around forever.

She came out a minute later, wearing a T-shirt and sweats, and her hair was up in a messy bun. Her eyes were red and puffy, a fact that I registered physically as a sucker punch to the gut. *Christ.* I'd made her cry, and by the looks of it, I'd made her cry a lot.

"Babe." I stood up, but she warily kept her distance, circling me and standing near the kitchen.

"I was going to call you," she said. "I got sick last night, so I came here. I didn't want you to catch it."

That was a lie, and I knew it. The way her chin jutted toward me, her eyes glittering in defiance, didn't match her apologetic tone.

"Why didn't you call me?"

"I was too sick. I just went to bed."

"Were you crying because you were sick?"

Blake frowned and wiped her eyes. "I wasn't crying."

I sighed and dropped back down on the couch.

"You should go." She wrapped her arms around herself. "I'll meet you at the apartment in a little while. You shouldn't be here."

"Why not?"

"Because our apartment's gross, and I'm ashamed to have you here." Tears shone in her eyes, but she stubbornly held them back.

"You have nothing to be ashamed of." I wanted to reach out and pull her to me, but I could tell by her stance that she wouldn't allow it.

"What about you, Lucas?" She wiped her eyes again. "Do you have anything to be ashamed of?"

"Are you talking about your sister?"

She gave an almost imperceptible nod. "I saw her last night, coming out of your office."

"Last night, right before you got sick?" I asked.

She nodded miserably.

"That's because she came to my office to try to extort money from me. And I gave it to her." I raked my hands through my hair. "But I also made her sign a contract that she'd stay out of our lives forever, and an airtight confidentiality agreement."

"I told you not to do that—she won't ever leave you alone."

I looked at her, silently pleading for her to forgive me. "I'm sorry that I gave her money, because I know that's not what you wanted. But I had to make a quick decision, and I chose to protect you, because I will *always* choose to protect you. Even if I've done a crappy job of showing you that thus far. I wanted her to leave us alone."

Now a tear slipped free, and she wiped it away roughly. "You said 'us.'"

I melted toward her. "Of course I did. Just because I'm an asshole doesn't mean I'm a *total* asshole."

"I told you, go home." She sniffed. "We don't even have to talk about this. It doesn't matter. We signed a contract, and I'm going to keep up my end—that is, if you want me to."

I yearned to pull her into my arms, but I had to tell her the truth. "The thing is you don't have to. The terms of the trust are being annulled. So I'm going to inherit my share of the money, probably in the next few weeks."

Blake looked as though she might pass out. "O-oh." She leaned against the wall to steady herself. "So you don't need me anymore."

I couldn't take it. I closed the distance and brought her into my arms. "That's not true. I realized it last night when you were gone. You're a total market disruptor, Blake."

She was stiff in my arms. "I'm sorry?"

I kissed the top of her hair. "You solved my must-have need."

She shook her head. "I don't understand what you're saying."

"Then let me explain it to you. Let me take you on a date before we go and get divorced."

BLAKE

"Where are we going?" We'd said a quick good-bye to my mother, with Lucas promising to be in touch soon. After we'd both showered and changed clothes, Lucas threw together an overnight bag and hustled me into the car.

"You'll see soon." He smiled and reached over, taking my hand and squeezing it. He hadn't said much, but he'd kept his hands on me since we'd been back together, making me feel wanted, making me feel confused. Even though he said we didn't need to be married anymore, he'd come back for me.

And as evidenced by the grin on his face, he seemed really, really freaking happy that I'd gone willingly.

We drove out of the city. Lucas was quiet but still

holding my hand. "Will you *please* tell me where we're going?" I asked.

He smiled at me, flashing that damn dimple. "I have a promise to keep," he said cryptically. If I hadn't been so happy that he'd come back for me and was holding my hand, I would've smacked him.

After almost an hour, Ian turned off at a sign for Hanscom Field. "We're flying somewhere?" I asked.

The dimple peeped out again.

"What? *What?*" The suspense was killing me. Then Ian pulled up right next to a lot filled with helicopters. Lucas donned a pair of aviator sunglasses and handed a pair to me, too. Suddenly, I understood. "We're flying in your helicopter?"

"Next stop, Seal Harbor." Lucas leaned over and kissed me on the cheek. "You look hot in those sunglasses, by the way."

He brought me to a beautiful blue copter and ushered me inside. After he harnessed me in and explained the safety precautions, he put on his headset. He started talking to the aviation tech, and I just watched his handsome profile. *So beautiful.* I loved every line on his face. I'd been lying to myself when I'd thought this could ever go back to being just a job.

He said he wanted to protect me. I wasn't sure from

what exactly, but I'd never had someone say that to me before. It made me feel safe, treasured, and loved.

Maybe it was finally time for me to be brave, to take a chance. To risk... everything.

"Lucas," I said, as he started up the engine.

"What, babe?"

"I love you!" I shouted over the noise.

He gave me a thumbs-up.

Ugh. I sulked in silence for the rest of the trip, looking at the beautiful scenery as we flew to Maine. It was very loud inside the copter, so we both had headphones on. "Babe," I saw Lucas mouth at one point, "are you okay?"

I just gave him a thumbs-up.

Later, after we'd flown over miles of green forest, as far as the eye could see, he started to descend. I could see a tiny airstrip coming up with a lone helipad. He headed toward it and landed the copter expertly. After he'd turned off the motor and taken his headphones off, he looked at me with an excited glint in his eye. "Babe?"

"Yes?"

"Welcome to Maine." He opened his door but then turned back. "And babe?"

"Yes?"

"I love you, too."

I felt my cheeks heat up. "Well, thank you for letting me know!"

He came back into the cockpit and pulled me close, crushing his lips to mine until I was dizzy. "Anytime, Mrs. Ford. Anytime."

Unlike on the islands, no driver was waiting for us, just Lucas's old Jeep SUV. He threw our bag into it, and we drove through Bar Harbor on a tiny highway, over a bridge and across a bay. Seagulls and eagles soared together over the dark water. With the windows down, the sea air blowing through my hair, and Lucas at my side, I finally felt something I'd never felt before: truly happy.

Realizing this, I laughed out loud.

"What's so funny?" he asked.

I shook my head. "I just feel relieved. I thought things were done with us. I didn't know what was going to happen, and I felt like my insides were being ripped out."

He nodded. "I got pretty drunk last night," he admitted.

"I got totally drunk last night."

"I missed you," he said simply and reached over to squeeze my hand.

"I missed you, too." I paused for a minute, watching the signs for lobster pounds and kayak rentals roll by. "What happened with my sister?"

"You don't want to know."

"Yes, I do. I don't want any secrets between us."

He groaned. "She came to my office in an, er, *formfitting* dress. She asked me for money. In exchange, she offered to have an affair with me—"

"Argh! She's a word that rhymes with blunt! I'll rip her eyes out!"

"—to which I said a loyal *no thank you*," Lucas continued. "Then she threatened to blackmail me by telling anyone who would listen that you're an escort. So I agreed to pay her," Lucas explained.

"But didn't you know last night that the trust terms were probably void?"

"Yes."

"So why did you care if she said things about me?"

He squeezed my hand. "Because I vowed to love, honor, and obey you. I didn't think I'd be honoring you too much if I let your trashy sister expose you all over social media. I thought you'd want to keep your past private. As do I—for personal reasons, not monetary ones."

"Thank you." I felt choked up. "How much money did you give her?"

Lucas shrugged. "Not that much."

"*Lucas*—"

"Five million dollars."

I started to splutter. "Five million!"

"Five million dollars, and I made her sign a contract saying that she'll never come after you again, and that she understands this is all the money she's ever going to get out of me. And I made her sign a confidentiality agreement. I figured it was easier this way. It might even be less expensive, if you take into account the fact that we most likely don't have to buy her Christmas, birthday, and housewarming gifts after what she's pulled."

I leaned my head back against the seat. "That's *insane*."

"You know me"—he grinned—"always throwing money at my problems."

During the rest of the ride through the rugged, beautiful Maine countryside, Lucas told me about what had happened with the trust and the lunch he'd had with Serena. "I think she still has a thing for Robert," he said.

I agreed. "She definitely still has a thing for Robert. She was all drunk and moony about him at our wedding."

"Good to know." If I ever needed to dangle something over Serena's head, which I probably would, it was good to have something to dangle.

We followed the signs to Seal Harbor and finally pulled into a long private drive. An enormous house became visible, with a wraparound deck on each floor. "Wow," I said. "Just... wow."

Lucas brought me into the house, and I was stunned by the spiral staircase and the floor-to-ceiling stone fireplace in the living room. There were Oriental rugs, bookcases teeming with books, and bright, gleaming hardwood floors. "This is amazing."

"Come here." Lucas held out his hand for me and led me onto the back deck. Northeast Harbor spread out below us, dotted with sailboats, yachts, and lobster boats. The mountains of Acadia surrounded the harbor. The view was breathtaking.

"I could get used to this," I said.

Lucas pulled me against him. "I hope so."

We spent the next hour on the deck, relaxing and holding hands, each of us nursing a glass of wine. "Martha Stewart has a house up here," he said.

"No way! Have you ever seen her?"

"Yep. Out to dinner one night at this Mexican place. She's as lovely in person as she is on television."

"Wow," I said, "a real celebrity!"

"I'm trying to keep you in the know. Maybe you'll see her up here, someday." His phone buzzed, and he checked it. Whatever he read made him choke on his wine.

I pounded him on the back. "What's the matter?"

Lucas gave one final cough. "I forgot about something—the Four Seasons."

"Huh?"

Lucas took another healthy sip of wine. "Back to the no secrets thing. I forgot to tell you—Elizabeth called me this morning."

My eyebrow shot up. "Why?"

"She said she wanted to, er... *see* me."

I crossed my arms against my chest. "*See* you? Or see you and then something more?"

"The latter. It kind of came out of the blue, but I think she heard about the inheritance and got kind of... excited."

"That witch! I knew she still wanted—"

"I thought that my father should know," Lucas said, interrupting me gently. "So I asked her to send me naked pictures of herself and to meet me at the Four Seasons this afternoon. Except that I'm not there—Ian is. And he just took a picture of her—that's what he texted me. I wanted documentation to prove it to my father, once and for all, that Elizabeth can't be trusted."

Blake held her hand out. "Hand me your phone."

Lucas shook his head, looking very wary. "I don't think that's a good idea, babe."

"The phone, *babe*. Now."

He gave it to me reluctantly. I scrolled through the

pictures and immediately wished I hadn't. I hopped up and paced the deck as I looked at them. "The nerve! Disgusting! What is she doing with that *cucumber*?"

"That one's my favorite. Classic." Lucas was laughing until I stopped him with a death look.

I tossed him back his phone. "Rich people are so weird."

Lucas motioned for me to come to him. "Except me."

"Right." I leaned down and kissed him. "Except you."

He looked up at me. "Listen, there's one more thing."

"Ew," I said, eyeing his phone warily. I didn't need to see any more of Elizabeth.

"It's not an *ew*. It's an *ooh*. Hopefully." He got up from his chair and took my hands.

And then he got down on one knee.

"Blake, we came at this in a non-traditional way." He looked up into my eyes.

"You bought me," I said.

"I bought you. The thing is, after I realized that I didn't technically 'need' you anymore and that I was going to let you go—that's when I realized that I really needed you. And that I couldn't let you go."

I squeezed his hands and fought back tears.

"That's what I was trying to tell you at your mother's. You are my total market disruptor. You're the thing that's changed everything for me. I can't go back to the way life was before you. I've evolved. You've evolved me." His thumb stroked my knuckles. "And I love you for it. I *love* you, Blakey."

"I love you, too." I let the tears fall. We weren't hiding anything anymore.

"So, will you marry me? Again?"

"Of course I will. Do you mean it?"

He stood up and pulled me into his arms. "Of course I mean it. I mean it so much, I invited your mother, my dad, Serena, Robert, Jake, my cousin James and his wife, Nikki and your other friends—hell, I even invited Elena —up here this weekend so that we could renew our vows. Because even though you're already my wife, I want you to know that I really want you to be my wife."

"Oh. Wow." My shoulders shook as I cried. "You're the one."

"That's right, babe. I'm the one. And you're the one for me."

EPILOGUE

LUCAS

Turks and Caicos

Three Years Later

"Pull up over there." I motioned toward an inlet.

"Are you sure you want to do this?" the captain asked.

"Yeah, are you sure you want to do this?" my father asked. He was sitting on the boat, next to his new wife, Cindy, who was twenty years his junior—a respectable fifty-something.

At first, he'd refused to divorce Elizabeth, even after I'd shown him the pictures and informed him that she'd shown up at the Four Seasons to go to bed with me. She'd met Ian instead, and much to her chagrin, he'd taken a picture of her as proof.

My father, dirty old man that he was, initially said

he thought it was sort of hot… But eventually, I think he realized that he wasn't going to be able to keep up with her and her varied, insatiable, and morally questionable appetite. So now he had a Cindy, and they played golf together. I even thought my mother would approve.

"Yes, I'm sure!" I barked. Blake eyed me nervously but loyal as ever, said nothing.

Serena sniffed. "You don't have to be rude to Dad." Robert wrapped an arm around her and shushed her. "Stop telling me to be quiet!" She laughed as he nuzzled her face and shushed her again. They'd been remarried for almost two years, but they were still acting like newlyweds.

We'd invited everyone to come out to the island for vacation. In addition to my father, Cindy, Serena, and Robert, Blake's mother was back at the house watching the baby, Lou, while she napped. Our two-year-old, Fletcher, was on the boat with us. Jake and Nikki had each respectively begged off for undisclosed reasons. They'd both been suspiciously avoiding our calls since the senate had resumed its session.

James and Audrey said they had three baseball tournaments and a banquet to attend, so they couldn't make it, either.

I'd invited Shirley, who was now my vice president

of operations, but she and her husband were currently vacationing in Scotland on the *Outlander* tour.

Thankfully, Chelsea was in Texas, auditioning for *The Bachelor Pad,* and couldn't come either. She'd given the last guy on *The Bachelorette* a rose, but they ended up at an impasse. She was still on the hunt for Mr. Right-and-Rich. She and Blake had made a sort of peace, at Blake's mother's teary request, when we'd had Fletcher. I didn't have to like it, but as Blake's husband, I *did* have to pretend to support her.

I grabbed the spear gun and ignored everyone. "Daddy!" Fletcher, cried, looking afraid of the thing.

I laughed and ruffled his hair. "Don't you worry. Daddy is an *expert.* At *everything.* Just ask Mommy."

Blake came over, taking Fletcher's chubby hand and watching nervously as I climbed down the ladder and precariously balanced the spear gun. "You don't have to do this," she whispered, "Not for me. I've made my peace with Dwayne. That was the day I knew you loved me."

I snorted. "That fish scared you, and I'm going to pay him back. He's been terrorizing French Cay for years!"

Fletcher's face puckered, as if he were about to cry.

"Don't worry, honey. Daddy isn't going to hurt the fish," Blake lied. "He just wants to go see him."

Fletcher shot her a look that cried *bullshit,* but he took after me, so he was smart and didn't say anything.

Or maybe it was because he was just two, I couldn't be sure. He watched me solemnly as I climbed down the ladder and adjusted my mask. Then I let go and, clutching the spear gun, went under the aqua waves.

I snorkeled toward the reef. There were thousands of brightly colored fish. I spotted puffers and parrotfish, an eel, and a stingray.

No sign of Dwayne.

He could be dead by now, I reasoned. Barracuda could live as long as fifteen years, but we'd first seen him three years ago. He'd been a legend then. Maybe he'd gone to barracuda heaven.

I looked for a long time, crisscrossing the surface near the reef and occasionally diving down. When I still didn't see him, I had to admit defeat. Mostly because I didn't want to scare poor Fletcher and worry Blake. I reluctantly headed back for the boat. Just as I was about to surface, I thought I saw a flash of silver, but when I turned, it was gone.

If that was you, you old goat... thank you. Because the afternoon that Dwayne had scared the bejeebles out of Blake was the afternoon I was sure I loved her. I'd had an inkling before, but that was the day I still thought of when I looked back at the beginning.

I still wanted to put a spear through him, though. So I could mount him on my wall.

"No luck," I said, climbing the ladder. I pulled off my mask and handed a relieved-looking captain the unused spear.

"Aw, honey, that's too bad," Blake said, rubbing my arm.

"I might hire someone to come out here and try to find him—" I started.

"But you won't," Blake continued for me, "because you've evolved."

"Right. Thank you for evolving me, Mrs. Ford."

She grinned at me, which still gave me a thrill. "Anytime, Mr. Ford. Anytime."

ABOUT THE AUTHOR

USA Today Bestselling Author Leigh James is currently sitting on a white-sand beach, nursing a Mojito, dreaming up her next billionaire.

Get ready, he's going to be a HOT one!

Full disclosure: Leigh is actually freezing her butt off in New Hampshire, driving her kids to baseball practice and going grocery shopping because her three boys eat non-stop. But she promises that billionaire is REALLY going to be something!

Visit her website at www.leighjamesauthor.com to learn more. Thanks for reading!

ALSO BY LEIGH JAMES

The Escort Collection

Escorting the Player

Escorting the Billionaire

Escorting the Groom

Escorting the Actress

My Super-Hot Fake Wedding Date

Silicon Valley Billionaires

The Liberty Series

Printed in Great Britain
by Amazon

68786024R00182